Breathing God

Michel Sauret

To Russ
May the Lord
Breathe though
you
~Michel
Sauret

PublishAmerica

Baltimore

First printing

ISBN: 1-4137-7737-6
PUBLISHED BY PUBLISHAMERICA, LLLP
www.publishamerica.com
Baltimore

Printed in the United States of America

A WORD FROM THE AUTHOR

I've had a lot of fears while writing this book. I've hesitated maybe too often in the development of these pages, and in a way I'm glad because good things come with time and patience. I hope that this novel proves true in that regard.

My fears in writing this book have ranged from the simplest, such as "What if I never finish this?" to fears of much more complexity: "What will it mean if I *do* finish it? Will it be a success? Will it be a failure?" I've asked myself these same questions and more since the day I started working on this, building up so much anxiety and worry that ultimately—and strangely—they exploded with joy when I knew that I had finally finished the very last page. But the biggest worry that I've had was maybe the most important one: What if this book offends God?

That question still hits my chest hard every time I think about it, so much so that the impact has filled my eyes with tears before. I've asked that question to my Bible study teacher, Judy Steidel—possibly the most inspiring and loving person I've ever met in my life—and her answer was simple.

"Pray about it," she said.

When she told me this, I decided to put my work away for a while—a period that ended up lasting over two months—and I prayed for its sake, asking God to guide my fingers to type the right words, and to help me accomplish something that He would be proud of me for.

I was seventeen when I first typed the initial words to this novel, and if that thought doesn't make you laugh or at least giggle then I'm not sure what will. I knew then what I wanted the book to be about, but it wasn't until I was almost finished with it, and after I had prayed for days and nights for guidance, that I realized that a large portion of this novel didn't correspond with the predictions that the Bible makes on the second coming of Christ.

Again I grew scared. I was even terrified because I might have to rewrite all the pages that seemed wrong. This time I turned to my father, a man whom I respect tremendously for his wisdom and knowledge on theology, and I asked him what I should do.

"Well, what kind of book is it?" he had asked me.

"It's a fiction book."

"Then let it be fiction," he said, "but keep it true." That answer relieved my heart, and immediately I understood what he meant. I knew then that it didn't matter so much that the events in this novel don't follow along with the predictions of Revelation. Partially this is because no one truly knows exactly what Revelation says. We may know the general idea, but we will never know for sure until the final day that we await for actually comes. In fact, Revelation isn't intended to tell us *how* Judgment will unfold—especially because it is filled with so much symbolism and hard-to-grasp images— but more importantly that we should be *ready* for it. In our actions, in our thoughts, and most importantly in our faiths we need to be prepared and know that we can stand before God without fears of our past. What became more important to me then was for my novel to accomplish a theme that keeps true to God, and I knew that the rest would be all right even if *factually* wrong.

This story, after all, is fiction.

Another part that contributed to my anxieties was the very first chapter. The development of this chapter is shocking, not just because it is built up with suspense, but because the thoughts that go through Jeremy's head (our hero) are vulgar and even distasteful. For this, I apologize to anyone who is offended, but I also want to explain that for this novel to work I *needed* Jeremy to be vulgar and I *needed* him to be who he is in this story.

My goal was to show how God loves us as individuals, no matter how great our faults, nor how far away we have gone from this love. God wants us to come back to him regardless of our mistakes. He sends out his Shepard to find his lost sheep. Jeremy is God's lost sheep. In writing this novel, I wanted to discover for myself what it took for a sheep this lost to be found again. Some huge miracles happen in the process, and I wanted to prove to myself and to my readers that even Jeremy—a young man who will offend you and maybe even disgust you from the very first few pages—can be used by God to fulfill his work.

So my apologies to you are honest and sincere, and I pray that you don't stop reading after just the first chapter. I pray that you go on to discover the beauties that can surface despite the vulgarities. And of course, I pray for you, for your family, and for your health because I want to thank you personally for buying this book.

— Michel Sauret

DEDICATION

Dedicated to Judy Steidel, who has taught so many young adults what it means to be Christian.

AWAKENING

Chapter 1

My eyes burst open like windows desperately trying to draw in fresh air. I wake up gasping, a sound resembling a choked off scream. My lungs heave, sucking thinly and wheezing. Suddenly, all at once, in a rush of a condensed breath, my chest expands to the farthest stretch of my skin. A moment ago I felt like I was suffocating, or worse yet drowning on internal liquids, my lungs filled to the brim in fluid. Now all I can manage is a ration of slow and deep breaths.

Long, dripping streams of sweat run from my face, reaching down the entire length of my body. My shaggy hair clings to my forehead like a wet mop. I wipe my face with my long sweatshirt sleeve, but even my clothes are drenched.

It takes me a moment to realize that I'm lying on a softly carpeted ground. I look around and notice that I'm occupying the center stage in front of the altar of St. Regis' Church. What seem like hundreds of faces look back at me with curious expressions, tainted by shock. An old man with a cane is shaking terribly, his cane rattling a droned vibration on the floor. He swallows hard. A lady no younger than him presses her hand on his shoulder, and he manages to hold the cane still. The church falls to silence.

A swarming headache screams from within my skull. It drills inside of my head, filling my blurring vision with streaks of light. My vision stammers, and I'm about to collapse back down to the ground, when suddenly my whole body convulses in a jerk. The crowd of people jumps at the motion, startled by it. I blink once, then again, squeezing my face tightly each time. A second passes, and a blur warps my vision for an instant, then it goes back to normal.

My heart pounds at my chest from within as if it were trying to get out. Terror strikes me, accompanied hand-in-hand by confusion.

What am I doing here?

I try to sit up a little, and for a second the headache takes a step up in its blurring effects like a carnival ride spinning faster and faster. All the while my breathing becomes only heavier and deeper. With each breath, my chest expands and contracts in heavy pumps. I cough up a nasty burst of air, and swirls of saliva escape along with it.

The entire front row of people is still, and I assume the same follows with the rows behind. They all watch me intently with open eyes and dropped jaws. There isn't a single stir of movement anywhere. Hundreds of eyes just stare at me as if they were watching some horrible disaster. A few people are holding one another, and small children embrace their mothers as tightly as they can. Their faces are mixed up. Most are stunned with bewilderment, while others can't seem to contain their terror.

A small child with short curly hair begins to cry, cutting away from the silence. His mother holds him tighter, trying to shush him. It's a soothing hush that leaves her lips, powerful even within its own quivering fright.

Over my right shoulder the priest clutches onto a heavy Bible as if he would sink without it. His expression is no different from the rest. As I turn to get a better look at him, he takes a frightened step backwards, almost tripping over the gown—or whatever—that drapes down to his feet. His round eyeglasses are poised on his nose at a crooked angle. His lips and jaw tremble. This makes his glasses twitch a little on his nose.

What just happened? Why am I the center of their complete, undivided attention?

Inside of my body, my stomach and intestines churn as if trying to disentangle themselves from one another. They're twisted in a knot that even a scout would have trouble meddling with.

Through all this, I haven't moved much more than my waist. Here and now, all I want is to walk back to my seat—or better yet, run out—but I can't even bring myself to my feet.

Now think. Since you can't move, at least try to think. Start with what you know.

Today is Sunday. I know that much just by looking around. Among the crowd, I spot out my grandma whom I came with today, just like all the past Sundays. She, like the rest, stares at me in a motionless gaze.

Think. Think!

What the hell's going on?

Start with today. Start with this morning. And suddenly I remember—not everything—but enough. My grandma and I were walking to the entrance of this church from the parking lot. She wore her mimic fur coat and fake leather gloves. Cruelty to animals is a cruelty to ourselves, she's always said. Her heels—one nearly falling apart—clicked and clacked on the stern, cold ground. On her face she didn't wear much make up; just a little blush toned her pale cheeks with rouge. Her narrow eyes were warm in themselves, seeming to hold smiles of their own. Her real name is Katherine Elisa Christ—by marriage—but I've always called her Gammy ever since I was little.

Every bitter Sunday, Gammy drags me to church. She knows I don't share her same beliefs, and I know that no matter what I do or say, every Sunday I *still* end up here regardless. It's a trade in a way. She takes care of me, and in return I accompany her here once a week.

As we walked with quick steps our breaths condensed into warm clouds. Winter still lingers outside. It doesn't care that we're now in April, and that it should've been replaced by spring by now. Clumps of dirty snow still grip the ground outside here and there, mocking us with their ugly presence.

As always, this morning we were late. I held the door open for Gammy to get her inside quicker.

"Thank you, Jeremy. You're such a gentleman," she'd said, as she gently plucked the gloves off her hands, finger by finger.

We walked inside the church, scrubbing our dirty feet on the mat, and shook off the last shreds of cold that clung to our clothes. Walking up the center aisle in search of a seat for two, I could sense everyone's eyes watching us. Faces and necks turned to follow our steps. I heard whispers, and the hair on the back of my neck stood on ends. I shot a gleaming stare over my shoulder, where suddenly a conversation stopped. The priest, who had already begun the service, offered a meek smile at us. He waited for us to find our seats, and then he went on. He and Gammy exchanged a glance; he nodded his head, and then continued on with his chants.

He spoke a few phrases, and the crowd responded.

The good thing about coming here late is the reward of a shorter mass.

11

Then the priest preached "the word of the Lord" as he calls it, and I leaned back in my seat. I looked around, watching this lost audience speak in unison, "The Gospel according to…"

—whoever. I didn't care. Really I wasn't even paying attention. Instead, my mind began its wandering, searching for something better to entertain my thoughts.

In the next aisle over to my left I saw a smoking-gorgeous brunette with her legs crossed. Her skin was somewhat pale, but its smoothness allowed for streaks of light to dash over it in a way that caught my eye. I followed the trace of light from her toes up to her thighs. Covering her thighs, she wore a tight miniskirt that was small enough to be stuffed in one's mouth—quite handy if you were in the process of role-playing. She had taken off her coat and set it down to her side, revealing a skimpy white tank top that showed off a mouthful of cleavage and a pair of visible, piercing nipples.

How girls can pull off wearing so little clothes when it's barely forty degrees outside, I'll never understand. But they seem to know exactly what they're doing, especially Catholic girls. They have a way of pulling just the right strings, and flipping all the obvious switches.

She looked over at me and gave me a quick smile. Her bleach white teeth gleamed between her lips as if she knew what I was thinking. I winked at her, and she looked away with an even bigger smile. She pinched on the edges of her skirt and pulled it down a little.

Tease.

She reminded me of a girl I met Friday night at my house during a party I threw. Her name was Trisha, or Terry…I forget. Her name isn't important. But I do remember every other detail of her naked body, grinding and pumping against my own.

Anyway, Trisha or Terry…no wait, Tara—that's what it was. How did I forget? I must have screamed her name at least a dozen times when we were together. Funny thing is that she screamed her own name, too.

She was a fun one.

So what if she was a little drunk and I took advantage of her? Everybody does it. And it's not like she didn't enjoy it. She moaned so loud that my friends could hear her over the music. Some even heard us from outside. Good thing Gammy wasn't home. After we were done, she ran to the bathroom and threw up chunks of liquor mixed in with

12

undigested foods. The color was peachy. The smell, on the other hand, was not. Once she was finished, I went to the toilet and flushed the condom we had used. She was sprawled with her arms over the edge of the bathtub, wearing nothing but her red panties. No thong unfortunately.

Drops of water fell from the showerhead and plopped on the back of her head. I woke her up, told her to brush her teeth, and had her go down on me for seconds.

It was a good night.

I think I still have her number somewhere, maybe in one of my drawers. Who knows—who cares. Not like I'm going to call her. She was a spur of the moment type of thing. There was no passion or "love" in it. I just wanted to have fun, and she seemed more than willing to help out. Really, Tara was no more than a rebound girl.

Just two days earlier my girl, Megan Scott, had dumped me. "We should see other people," or some other shit along that line, she had said. She was always looking for other people, even when we were together.

"So we're through?" I had asked her, picking at something under my fingernails.

"You can still call me."

"Yeah, I probably won't."

Then Friday night, there she was at my house with all her friends, holding one of the many beers that she would down that night. I saw her looking at me, so I looked away. I looked for a good score, a pretty girl, and a little fun for the night. After all, it had been *her* idea to look elsewhere.

Moments later, after my mind had finally finished with its wandering, the preacher spoke up. "Let us rise and join in hymn," he said while raising his hands, calling us to stand. Quite oppositely, I kicked back and relaxed. I made myself comfortable in my bench and put my elbows out to my sides. After all, this is the "house of God," and I'm his invited guest. Gammy gave me a stern look, but I paid no attention to it. Slowly my neck started to tilt back, and without knowing it, I had fallen asleep.

And that's all I can remember. Having thought back to all that hasn't cleared anything up. Again, I look at the crowd dumbfounded, hoping to draw in any clue that they're willing to give me.

None.

Everyone is still the same immobilized statue they were before.

Struggling, I stand up, turning to the priest. He takes another frightened step backwards, holding onto his huge Bible even tighter. I gulp a thick chug of saliva, which feels thick and curdy in my throat. The priest's jaw stammers, emitting cut off sounds that aren't even half words. Wearily, in a soft voice I ask, "What's going on?" My voice sounds childish and slightly immature. It sounds so innocent and scared.

A silent moment passes and I feel like screaming at the top of my lungs. Finally, he works up the courage to speak and, in a soft, enchanted voice, he whispers, "You...you flew."

Chapter 2

Their eyes keep staring at me with a silent judgment befalling them. A flush of heat rises up to my neck, wrapping around my throat like a burning hemp rope. I chug hard at a gulp of saliva, which jams at the level of my Adam's apple for a long, suffocating moment. My eyes close slowly, shutting away their stares to a hushed darkness. I'm imagining this, I try to convince myself. Yet, when I open them again, nothing changes. They stare at me as if I were some kind of a freak accident left behind by the circus.

I want to scream at them. I just want to scream, and scream, and scream until my lungs feel like they're breathing hot sand, but the choking sensation won't let go of its grasp. The words I intend on yelling become clogged, forming a bulge in my throat. *Quit looking at me! What did I do to you?* But I can't say any of it. My lips are pressed shut, refusing to speak.

My heart is still pounding at my chest like a hard knock at the door, though its beat has slowed. With what little strength I can gather, I take a step down from the sanctuary. A wave of tingly pinpricks rises up my legs, shooting up from each foot that steps forward. As I limp down the aisle, the crowd of people makes way. Their drawn, still faces follow me, their necks turning, and a few of their lips gasp with amazement.

They all spread out without objection, pushing out to the sides. I come close to brushing up against a middle-aged woman, when I hear her squirm and draw away. The rest of them breathe heavily, pressing back—trying to avoid my touch.

Outside, I scamper around the corner and slouch down on a curb besides a tall pile of smoky-gray snow. If I had the keys to Gammy's car, I would take off and go. I don't want to see that same look on her face again.

15

My hands tremble and I know it's not because of the cold. My palms feel damp and sweaty, as if I just shook hands with the devil himself. I wrap my fingers around my knees to keep them still, but they, too, are hit hard with jitters. My right foot twitches, and the spasm shoots up to my thigh.

I try to let my mind wander away from this enigma, but I can't. Except it's not an enigma. Obviously the people inside know exactly what happened. *They* know why they were looking at me—I don't, and I don't want to ask. I'd rather not know than to deal with any one of their faces ever looking at me again.

I just want Gammy to come out so that I can go home.

Thinking back to what the priest said to me, I know it doesn't make any sense. And yet, I'm trying to find a reason for why it should, the same way a child tries to reason Santa's own defiance to logic.

You flew.

The words echo in my head without justification. Maybe he was confused and meant to say something else, and "You flew" was all he could get out. How could I have possibly flown? People don't fly!

Twenty more minutes pass on my watch in slow, unhurried ticks before finally the doors open. The crown streams out from inside slowly, holding unsure steps, in search of their cars. Their faces are full of excitement now, not at all resembling the expressions that I saw inside. They talk frantically amongst each other as if they just finished watching the blockbuster of the year.

An old couple passes by me, talking so fast that it's hard to catch everything they're saying. I crouch closer to my pile of snow, hidden from their sight. Their words mesh into one another, each one asking questions that the other doesn't seem to know how to answer.

"Who was that boy?" the old man asks energetically.

"What does it mean?" she says, without answering him.

"Surely that message wasn't for us, do you think? *We're* no hypocrites!"

"Of course not. I would be ashamed to admit it. But we should prepare all the same."

"Right, right. We should prepare." On that, they agreed.

More people come rushing out, trying to walk faster than those ahead of them. A group of younger kids walk on, all hurdled around one another. They seem to be gossiping amongst themselves.

"Did you see that!" a boy exclaims.

"We're not blind, Travis! Everyone saw it!" a freckled, red-headed girl answers the boy.

"I can't believe it. I can't even believe my eyes!" another puts in. Their eyes, glossy and distant, seem to be looking into a world across the sky.

Gammy follows behind, walking alone. A slim smile stretches her face, forming dimples in her cheeks. On her hands, held in front of herself with her fingers intertwined, she wears only one glove. She walks by and doesn't even see me.

"Gammy!" I call out to her, and she turns. Her smile widens. The wrinkles on her face seem deeper than ever before, but her eyes are joyous and bright. A tear seems to be clinging to the corner of each eye. Struggling for balance, I get up to approach her. She walks towards me.

"Are you okay? Are you all right?" she says.

"I'm fine," but it's the furthest thing from the truth. The word "nauseous" couldn't even begin to describe the way I feel right now. I feel like my stomach has just been through the rinse cycle of a laundry machine washer.

"You don't look fine. You're so pale," she says worriedly. I stumble for balance, and she catches me by the elbow. "Here, hold on to me."

"You can't hold me up, Gammy. I'm too heavy for you."

We take a few stumbling steps. Both of her hands try to support me by the elbow.

"Gammy, what happened in there?" I ask.

"I should be asking *you* that. How did you do it?"

"Do *what?*"

"What made you say those things?"

"I don't know what you're talking about, I really don't."

Then the crowd notices me. At first they hesitate, but then they start to approach us. Almost all at once, they circle around.

"What was his name again?" a blonde woman asks her daughter, whispering. I recognize the girl. She's the one who sat across the aisle from me inside the church.

"Jeremy, I think," she whispers back.

"Jeremy! Jeremy!" they begin to scream all at once. They rush towards me, bumping into one another to get to me first. Before, they didn't even want to be touched, but now they close in on me like desperate fans.

"Let's get out of here," I tell Gammy with a panicked voice. "I don't wanna be here. Let's go home. Now."

Understanding, Gammy grabs for my hand and leads me towards the car. Seconds later, I'm the one leading the way, moving faster than she can. She tries to keep up with my pace, struggling. I slow down for her, but only enough so that we can stay away from the crowd. I hop inside her old station wagon while she eases herself in slowly. She fumbles for the keys and then starts the ignition. By now the crowds have swarmed all around us. A few come right to my window and tap at the glass with their palms. Others are screaming for me hysterically, pounding at every side of the car. The rest wait a few paces behind in hope that I'd step out. No one, fortunately, stands to block the way.

They step back as Gammy pulls out slowly. As soon as they begin to clear the way, Gammy presses down on the gas harder. Leaving the parking lot, I look back at the crowd through the mirror. They just stand there, all grouped up, watching us leaving them behind.

Chapter 3

The ride home is quiet and uneasy. Every few seconds Gammy opens her mouth, turning to me, as if to say something, but then doesn't, and closes it again. Luckily the drive is short, and a few minutes later Gammy parks the car in front of our house. Immediately, I step out, without even waiting for her to put it in park.

"You forgot your jacket," she says after me.

"I'll get it later," I say with brisk puffs of air leaving my lips.

The street we live on is filled by two rows of cloned houses. It's like that mirror effect where you see yourself a couple hundred times before finally you're too small to be visible anymore. Instead of yourself here, it's the same house that's duplicated all the way down to the end of the street.

From one house to the next there's only a slim gap that extends in between. The gap is hardly wide enough for a person to walk through. In front of our house, there's not even enough grass to call it a yard. A strip of cracked stones that seep into the ground forms a walkway, leading to the steps of our front porch. Sometimes I look at my house and I think of a doll house, other times I see a robotic, squared face. It all depends on the curtains Gammy decides to drape that week. The paint on the porch of every other house on the street is chipped and cracking away. Ours, instead, is a celestial blue, which Gammy and I had painted just last summer. Our door is a sunset yellow comforting us with an invitation every time we return home.

As we step inside, our dog Romulus barks at us happily at our return. He wags his tail, whapping it against an old wooden coat hanger that stands for no other purpose than decoration. He spins around in circles inviting us to pet him. I approach to rub him on the head, but instead he leaps on me with his front paws. I stumble back, but I regain my balance quickly. I pat Romulus' head with my palm, and he sticks out his tongue, panting to show appreciation. Romulus has always been an overly excited dog, even for an Alaskan wolf. His eyes are a beautiful, icy blue color, and his coat is so soft that it puts plush teddy bears to shame. He drops back down on all fours and stars lapping at the water bowl with delicate licks. I look at my chest and notice that he left two dirty paw prints on my shirt.

"Jeremy, I don't even know where to begin," Gammy says with a tone that is half worried and half excited.

"Then don't," I say firmly, holding a smile that feels plastered above my chin.

"I've got so many questions that I—I don't know where to start."

"Let's not talk about it. I don't want to."

"Jeremy, come back here."

"Not now, I'm going to take a shower."

I lift my arms and sniff myself under my armpits. A raunchy scent that resembles dirty socks blended with garlic salt and rotten salmon comes up to sting my nostrils. It's the nastiest aroma my body has ever produced. All that sweat, I think. My clothes are still damp from it. I grab a towel from the closet and walk in the bathroom.

I step into the shower, turning the knobs, which make a squeaky metal sound. There's a creaking noise as there always is when turning on our faucets and showers, and then a jet of frigid water comes down on my face. My skin tenses up into thousands of goose bumps. I breathe heavily, panting, and I wait it off. My nipples turn into tiny marbles on my chest. Finally, after a few more seconds, warm water shoots down, allowing my body to relax.

I try to think about what happened in church, but I let it go. Freely and easily the warm water allows for my stresses to roll off my mind like steam lifting off the surface of a hot road. Within the water's warmth, a gentle touch seeps into my skin with each drop instead of bouncing or sliding down my body. I let its heat pull me to a single, quiet thought.

I dreamt of her again last night.

I suck the steam in through my nostrils before being pulled further. She was so beautiful. A long white gown extended down to her toes from her shoulders, and tiny angel wings reached out from her back. In the dream we stood in a bleach-white room where everything seemed to go on infinitely. Her gown camouflaged into the rest of the whiteness, except where the wrinkles of cloth created delicate shadows.

Her face was softened and it seemed to radiate with a gentle glow. Her eyes, deep and brown, sucked me out into their seeping grasp. Her nose was pinched in her face, small as a pea, it seemed. She smiled a thin, contended stretch of her lips. Barely ever did she grin showing teeth— even in some of her most enthusiastic moods her lips remained closed. Her tiny wings wriggled, and she clasped her hands in front of her.

I don't believe in angels, mainly because I don't believe in anything spiritual. God: doesn't exist. The Bible: just a story. Sin: a hell of a lot more fun than going to church. But I still envisioned her as an angel in that dream as in so many others I've had before. Besides, according to Gammy, when a person dies, they don't become an angel. They rise into Heaven in the form of a spirit. Gammy says that God created angels way before he created man.

Her skin looked alive and brilliant, as if even up in Heaven she still catches rays from the sun. She spoke to me in a voice that knew no turmoil. It was the same voice that she had often used to soothe me when I cried when I was little. But I don't cry anymore, and so I'm not privileged of that voice anymore except when my eyes are closed, and my mind is far away from reality. I'm all cried out. I don't think there's even a single teardrop left in me.

In the dream, I wasn't me. Not exactly, at least. In the dream I was only nine, still wearing that funny bowl-cut that every kid at some point of time has to be tortured with. My mom held my small hands in hers, gently but firmly, and spoke a single phrase. "Jeremy," she said, "you've been chosen."

Seconds later she took a swan dive into the whiteness and transformed into the color red. She became a large raindrop of blood. It was the same blood that I've seen before in my life, stretched out into puddles and puddles of the mirroring liquid. This was back when I was the same nine-year-old boy who I was in the dream: The Jeremy who didn't understand so was simply taught to *accept* instead.

In the dream my mom looked so sweet and so happy. Delicate, that's the word. That's not how I remember seeing her the last few minutes of her life. I remember her being so scared and confused. Decaying and violated.

21

The not-a-care-in-the-world Jeremy I was half of my lifetime ago was only nine and fragile. At that age—not even close enough to be an imprudent young teenager—I was exposed to the darker shade of reality. Ever since kindergarten I knew that different shades of crayon existed, except I'd always ignored the ugly, murky pastels to draw my pictures. That year, though, I became introduced to those muddy, dark colors in a manner that was more than personal.

It was night out and only a solitary moon existed in the sky. That big, round moon watched down upon us like an owl's eye. This was back when I believed that the moon came out at night to play. It followed me everywhere I went as my companion, and to make sure I was never left alone. Sometimes it would bring his tiny friends, the stars, and I would play together with them, imagining pictures and connecting the dots to form shapes. That night, though, only the moon came out. Maybe his buddies were too afraid, as they should have been.

My parents and I were driving back home from a Detriot Lions game. The Lions had won. I lounged freely in the back of my father's Cadillac, squeaking around with my pant legs rubbing against the leather seats. At one point, my dad had taken the wrong turn, distracted, and quickly we became lost. Soon we found ourselves in the eerie part of town, the part of town that I was so naïvely ignorant and unaware of; where junkies droop onto the street like hungry vampires looking to feed just after the sun comes down.

The more my dad drove, the more we seemed to get lost. The streets turned darker, and the buildings more dilapidated with each turn we took. We turned around another bend, our high beams piercing white rays through all the black, when an old man scampered away from the light, hiding behind a dumpster. The car stopped, and in front of us we saw a brick wall. It was a dead end, surrounded all around by more walls. My dad clicked the gage into reverse, and we began to pull back around. Then the car jerked, stopping all of a sudden. Behind us, two men stood with their shoulders sagging and their faces shadowed over flatly.

Then, another man showed up, stepping forward slowly. He approached my dad's closed window with steps that had no echo. His face was hard to make out at first, but then my eyes adjusted and slowly his features came to focus. From his neck to his chin he had a wide, gashing

22

scrape. His jaw was rounded over but blunt, with the ball of his chin jutting out like a dirty old man trying to peer in on an erotic view. His upper lip was thin, almost nonexistent, while his lower one pooched. That lower lip was chapped and crusty. His nose was regular, just like any nose, but it too was peeling off in dry flakes. Piercingly, his eyes peered down at my dad with a look I wasn't able to describe at the time. I had heard of the word "lust" before at youth group, but I didn't know that it applied to his eyes just then. His blond hair was ruffled and knotted. In a few places it seemed to be glued in clumps.

"Spare change?" this pale man asked in a sore, raspy voice. The other two began to approach my mother's side of the car and made disgusting faces at her. My dad ignored him with a dubious look on his face but didn't move nor lock the doors. "Spare change?" the man asked again more persistently, while knocking at the window. His fingers were so bony that his hands looked like bundles of twigs.

My dad was just about to drive back, when I tapped at his shoulder and stole away at his attention.

"What is it, Jeremy?" my dad said in an agitated tone.

"Daddy, he looks hungry. Why won't we give him some money?" But I didn't know. I was too young and uneducated to the disgusting shadow that this world holds when the sun goes down that I just didn't know. Before my dad could answer me, the pale, skinny man opened the door and pulled him out of his seat. My mother screamed, and I didn't understand that something bad was going on. How could I not see it happening as clear as day? Even though it was night, it should've been obvious to me! How did I not recognize the expressions on the three men's faces to be of greedy desire?

These were the three wise men who came to offer death to my parents and to my childhood. The gift of the three magi. Instead of giving, though, they were prepared to take, and take so much.

The other two men pulled my mother out, and she began to scream even louder. One of them muffled her voice with a scabbed, charcoal-covered hand. The hand looked so huge over her face. I screamed with my tiny voice for the men to stop, but they wouldn't listen. "I have two quarters!" I yelled for them. "I have two quarters! Just leave my mommy alone!" I was so innocent and so stupid that I did not know that fifty cents wasn't nearly enough to satisfy their greed.

The man without an upper lip began beating my father in the head with an iron pipe. My father didn't put up a fight. "To fight with fists is to ignore that you have a brain to use and words to speak," he had always said to me. I had always held that saying as a doctrine until that night. The pipe cracked down one last time with a hollowed sound, and my dad's body laid limp in the ugly man's grasp.

The man let go of him, and my dad lay on the ground unconscious. Streams of blood poured out of his face. *Please no*, my subconscious cried out to me in desperation. *Please don't find out about the cruelty of death and rape at such a young age. Please no!*

The blond man left my dad on the ground like a carcass handed over to the vultures, and joined the other two. Together they began to rip off my mother's clothes like an undeserved Christmas package, all too eager to wait till the twenty-fifth. She screamed in terror, calling for my dad, calling for me, calling for anyone willing to save her. I didn't know what they were doing to her, but soon I would realize it. I was about to find out how disgusting things turn when the sun goes down and there are no stars in the sky. That moon was no companion. It didn't follow me just so I would not be left alone. It was there to watch for things to turn their worst.

I screamed for my mommy, pounding my palms flat on the window. *Why are they hurting her?* I asked myself. *Why would they hurt my mommy?* My voice spoke nothing nearly as coherent. My voice just screamed. It collapsed with cries.

One of the three men choked my mother's throat with one hand while his other ripped her shirt open. I looked away and stepped out of the car from the side where I wouldn't be able to see her. Instead I saw my dad, lying dead on the ground.

Rather than running to help my mother, I ran away. I ran like the coward I was. I ran away from the truths of murder and rape, and the faster my feet stretched across the road's length, the quicker my youth died. With each footstep, a pang ran up my pounding legs, up my pounding spine, up to my pounding brain. An infinite number of blocks away I saw a policeman in his car. That's what I used to call pigs back then, back when I had respect for everything and anything. I told him what was happening and he rushed me to the deadly scene I had just tried to escape.

I wish he had brought me to the farthest place away possible, but instead he brought me right back to where my parents lay motionless on the engulfing ground. If it could have, that ground would have laughed sadistically.

The Cadillac was gone, but the two bleeding bodies were left behind. My father bled from the face, and my half-naked mother bled from between her legs. That horrifying image remains printed into my memory to this day. Right then I wished I had stayed with them instead of running away. I wished that the three ugly men had finished the rest of me off instead of just killing a part. I wished I had never offered those men my last two quarters.

The water in the shower heats up into a scalding hot vapor, biting me back to reality. It burns my skin and I jump out fast. Most of the soap is rinsed off except for a few clumps of shampoo suds behind my ears. I go to the mirror and hope to see that nine-year-old Jeremy I knew so long ago.

Instead, I just see me.

Chapter 4

It's Monday morning and I'm starting to feel a little bit better. A sense of relief has washed over me with the night's sleep. Gammy is in the kitchen, holding the morning newspaper in her lap while sipping on a cup of coffee.

I slip by the kitchen's entrance in hope that she doesn't notice me.

"Jeremy, come here a second," she calls out to me

"I can't. I'm going to be late for school," I say, and I rush out. That's a lie. First period doesn't start for another half hour, and it only takes ten minutes to get to school.

Outside, snow is falling hard. Maybe it's never going to stop, I think. I watch a few flakes reach the ground, then I lose my trace, distracted by all the other flakes coming down with the ones I was watching. Already the grass has been coated over thinly by a sheet of white.

I drive to school hoping that at least my classes will get my mind off of things. I step inside the main entrance, and the normally loud entrance hallway becomes silently dead. It takes a moment for this to happen; it doesn't just hush away all at once, and you can still hear the voices coming from the neighboring halls. More faces look at me with the same stares I witnessed yesterday. Their dull, wide eyes seem to try to extract something from me. The silence puts a knot back into my stomach, and brings my skin to a flushed heat that rolls over from one shoulder to the other like a spreading hot towel. Once again I'm challenged by another staring contest, knowing I'll lose and that I have nowhere to run. Even the guidance counselors have stepped out of their office to take a look.

A clustered group of the known Christian kids—whom I always see with tainted, fake smiles on their faces—seems afraid of me. A small huddle of kids with their hair dyed jet black and their faces pale and narrow look at me as if I just killed their lord, Satan. They're the Goths, as mostly anyone will announce their label. Rage builds up in me: a rage that covers up the fear that's actually simmering beneath.

"What the hell is everyone looking at?" I finally scream at their faces with my arms spread open. I try to look menacing, but I don't think I do a very convincing job. I walk past the crowd and everyone makes way. Not one person dares to block my path. Not one of them tries to touch me. With each step I take, another kid slides cautiously out of my way. I pass the small group of Goths and a guy wearing a trench coat follows me with angry eyes. I look at him in disgust.

"Morbid wannabe," I tell him. He sneers at me without saying a word.

I reach my locker and the crowds behind me pick up their chatter as if nothing had happened. I put down my book bag and I work my fingers on the lock. I turn the knob, stopping at each needed number and pop the metal tab. The locker doesn't open.

I spin the little wheel faster a couple times and try the combination again. It won't work. I can't concentrate. I try it again, but I still get the same result. A thick vein bulges out from the side of my temple, and I can feel it pumping blood heavily. I try the three numbers again.

Nothing.

"Well, feed a pigeon rice and fuck it up its ass! How come you didn't tell me about this?" a familiar voice asks from behind.

I spin the knob again, but it's useless. I can't get the locker open.

"Tell you about what?" I ask, turning to Ben Norton, who's holding a newspaper in his hand. Ben's black hair is spiked forward like sharp spears. His cheekbones are bold and his chin pointy, giving several sharp edges to his face. He has a long neck with a bulging Adam's apple. He's wearing a faded purple shirt that is much too tight for his body. In big, bold white letters the tee-shirt reads: "Proud Cheerleader Mom" with a picture of a megaphone below it. He bought the shirt at Goodwill for $2.99.

"About this," he tells me, smacking the paper with one hand.

I try the locker again, but it doesn't open. By now I don't expect it to. I groan heavily and punch the metal door with the side of my fist.

"Jeremy, did you take your pills today? Or maybe you took too many? Can you see straight? That's not your locker, buddy."

He taps the flat end of his finger at the locker number: 308. Mine is the next one over at 309. Inhaling deeply, I take a second to remember the combination that I just now performed what felt like an infinite number of times. I spin the knob once more, and the locker snaps open.

"What are you talking about, Ben? What's with the newspaper?" I ask him.

"Man, I thought we were best friends."

"We are, but what the hell are you ranting about?"

He gives me a skeptical look and holds the paper in front of me. I see a snapshot of me grinning on the front page, and I grab it.

"Just read," he says.

Christ Predicts Judgment Days
Is There a New Messiah Amongst Us?

DETROIT, MICHIGAN. This past Sunday, April 2, a strange event took place at the warm and welcoming Saint Regis' Catholic Church. According to over three hundred witnesses who attended mass that morning, eighteen-year-old Jeremy Christ—get this—levitated in the air and announced a catastrophic prediction through a voice that was not entirely his own. Yes, he physically flew, if that's not too hard to believe. The event left behind only shock and more confusion than anyone there seemed able to handle.

Some think that there is a new Messiah amongst us, and Jeremy's last name (Christ) only reinforces this belief. Others are skeptical and aren't willing to believe it.

When interviewed, twelve different churchgoers described the events that happened on Sunday. All their stories, although questioned separately, showed to tell the exact same story

Seventeen-year-old Margaret Allen stated, "When we all stood up to sing, he (Jeremy) began to jerk violently. He was convulsing. At first I though he was just faking it, like some sort of sick joke, but then it looked like he was having a seizure. Then he began to…" she paused for a moment, clearing her throat "…to lift right off the ground. He flew in front of our very eyes and moved to the front of the altar. Then he started to talk in a weird, deep voice. He said, 'Hypocrites! All of you, hypocrites! You come to Church this day as Christians, and then live the lives of sinners the rest of the week! Judgement is coming upon you. Which of you can say that you are prepared? Beginning on the first day of the seventh month of this year, your faiths will be tested for 40 days and 40 nights. Darkness will come to roam the Earth. Remain inside your households till the end of Darkness, I warn you! Only those of you who prove your faith will enter the Kingdom Come.'" Needless to say, Margaret seemed very agitated during the interview. Still, after her convincing description of events, it is hard to imagine someone floating in mid-air during Mass.

Father John Birmingham, who celebrated the Mass that Sunday, is convinced that it was an act of God. Some accuse him of having staged the event, but he states that he "had absolutely nothing to do with what happened to Jeremy in church on Sunday."

Jeremy's words carry a shocking message delivered to us. July (the seventh month) is not far away, and we have a few questions to face: Which of us will follow the message carried out by Jeremy? What can we expect from these forty days? And most importantly, do we have a new Christ amongst us?

I run my eyes back and forth through the article. Is this for real? Is this what really happened? No, it can't be. I was asleep. That's all. There was no miracle. There was no message. There was no *flying*!

You flew.

I read the story twice over, but the words make less and less sense each time that I read them. Ben stands there looking at me, with odd curiosity. I don't know what to say. All I did was fall asleep, and now *this!*

I look up at Ben from the newspaper, but his expression hasn't changed. I look down at the story again, and back up at him. I'm just waiting for him to say, "April's fool!" even though he'd be a couple days late. I'm just waiting for him to laugh and say, "You should've seen the look on your face!" But he doesn't. He keeps looking at me worriedly. It's a look that tells me that this isn't—as much as I'm begging it to be—a joke, after all.

Why me? How did this happen? No, that's what it is. It didn't. It never happened. This paper is bullshit!

I keep looking up at Ben with a gaped mouth. Finally he speaks. "You seem kind of surprised about this."

"*Kind of?*" I say. "'Kind of' isn't exactly the right phrase. I'm shocked out of my fucking mind! How do you explain this? How!?"

"How should I know? I didn't write this. You mean you didn't know about it until now?"

"No! All I remember is falling asleep. Then I woke up beside the altar covered in sweat, and—"

You flew.

"But—" Ben tries to argue.

"But nothing. This is bullshit!" I say, shaking the paper, "It *has* to be made up. They can't just write this crap! They can't expect me to play along with their little game." By now, I'm almost screaming. I don't even know if I'm angry or scared anymore.

"Jeremy, calm down. This isn't a fucking *National Enquirer* you're holding in your hand. This is a legitimate newspaper! It's a real story. About *you!*"

"No, you see, somebody is playing a dirty little joke on me. The paper says I flew! People don't *fly!* It doesn't happen. *This...*" I scream, shaking the paper in one gripped hand as if I was choking it, "this is make-believe!"

"Jeremy! There were *three hundred* people in the church when it happened. The author of this column can't bribe three hundred people to agree with what the paper says. It doesn't work that way."

He does have a point. I could go up to any one of those people who were at church, and they would all tell me the same story I just read. The paper couldn't be a fake because all those witnesses would expose it to be a lie if it were. Somebody wouldn't just make up a story when there are three hundred people who can easily disprove it. But that's the problem. I guess I'll never know for sure because I never want to see any of those faces again. I don't want to feel like a freak the way I did this morning and yesterday at church.

A sharp, penetrating ache shoots throughout my stomach, clenching my intestines tightly in its grasp. I feel my insides twisting and turning in on me, making me feel ill all over. I tongue at a sickening acid taste in my throat and cheeks. I swallow but the taste doesn't go away. I'm about to vomit—the feeling is one that I've had already too many times, and if I don't make it to the bathroom in time people will be picking up "Holy Spew" off the ground as a souvenir.

I run to the nearest bathroom, just beyond the long stretch of lockers, holding my mouth with one hand. In the other I'm still clutching the newspaper in a tight roll. I burst through the restroom entrance, and the door slams open. A tall kid jumps out of the way, barely missing the swing of the door.

"Hey!" he yells.

I shove him out the way, and his back strikes against the paper towel dispenser. I yank the door to the first stall, but it won't open. I rattle it hard until a wimpy voice tells me, "There's somebody in here!" I try the second one, and I pull it so hard that I almost fall backwards. I step in, and I begin to hug the toilet as if it were my new best friend. I hurl my morning breakfast—a muffin and a bag of white cheddar popcorn—into it, like blurting out all my secrets to my friend. The more I hurl into it, the more my contents splash into the water. I can feel vomit chugging up my throat and seep between my teeth. It has the same acidic taste I was tonguing just seconds before. It comes out yellow and thick.

Behind me, someone bangs at the stall from outside. I keep hurling, making noises only a young kid would find funny. "Hey, asshole!" the voice says. The john takes in more and more of what I've got to give, without complaint. The last chunks of vomit strain my throat, ripping at it like tiny rocks instead of soft half-digested food. It all splashes down into the contaminated water.

I wipe my lips with one wrist and stand up.

"You mind?" I say to the kid banging at the door. He's the guy I threw against the wall.

He takes one look at me and then his eyes widen. Fear strikes his face and he stumbles backwards, tripping over his own shuffling feet.

"You're that freak!" he says, pointing a shaky finger at me, and runs out.

"Yeah, that's right!" I scream after him. "I'm the Messiah who's going to bring vengeance upon you! Run! Run and scream in fear, or else I will strike you down with a lightning bolt!"

The other kid from the stall runs out, whimpering, his pants still halfway down his legs and a strip of toilet paper clinging to his ass.

Chapter 5

I don't know how I'm going to go through this day, but I guess I'll just have to manage. I'm trying to deal with this fucked up little joke whoever is playing on me. My skull feels like lumber being split in two by a hatchet. But I think I'll just have to play along. They tell me I'm a Messiah? Then I'll play the Messiah! But if I have to pretend to be a messenger from God, then I'll do it *my* way.

Why does my last name have to be Christ? Why couldn't I just be a Smith, or Bacon, or even Douglas? Or better yet, why didn't my parents just name me Jesus? *Nobody* in their right mind would accept a second Jesus Christ in the making. Nobody! If my name was Jesus, they wouldn't even bother paying attention to me. They would just laugh in my face and leave me the hell alone.

I walk through the halls, dealing with all of this, and nobody will touch me. Nobody will even speak to me. Going down the math hall I brush against some girl, and she starts screaming. She screams her little pea-brained head off and looks at her arm as if it were on fire. How can so many people read the news? How can so many of them recognize me?

"Go on!" I scream at her. "If you don't wash that off immediately, real soon your arm's going to fall off! And three days from now there's a good chance that it'll spread to your kneecaps. Who knows what's next from there? You just might be a gimp the rest of your life!"

She believes me. How can you not believe the Messiah? She runs to the bathroom to rinse her miserable, melting arm off.

I'm going to be at the center of the whole world's attention today, and there's nothing I can do about it. It seems that in this world, unless you're famous or rich you don't even exist, but as soon as you get your fifteen minutes of fame, then everyone's crowded behind you, wiping your ass with triple quilted toilet paper. It's sickening how it all works.

When my parents died, it seemed like I became the center of everybody's life. Everyone kept asking me questions. Everyone insisted on being around me. During the months that followed my parents' death, I met relatives I didn't even know I had. Everyone I knew pretended to care about me. It was a nightmare that I had to live over and over again until finally the news got old, and people moved on. It was then that I needed a helping hand. It was *then*, when I wasn't important anymore, that I needed to know that people cared. This is why I love Gammy so much. She was the only one who left me alone when everyone suffocated me with questions and sympathy, and then showed her love once the nightmare was over to everyone except me. She supported me through the years by taking me in her house. No questions asked. She was more than happy to take me in. She bought me clothes, fed me, and did everything else that a parent would. She never complained about me being a burden, and always, always made me feel welcome. Ever since, she's been the only one who understood me and really listened to what I had to say.

First period begins, and my calculus teacher pretends not to know anything. She knows. I know she knows. I can see it in her eyes. She's handing back our quizzes, and she doesn't even make eye contact with me. Her hand draws away quickly as I take the sheet from her hand.

On my paper I see a red C+. "Hey, teacher!" I shout after her. A few students shift in their seats, embarrassed for me. I've never called out any of my teachers like that before, but this felt satisfying, if not a bit deserved.

She turns, smiling a scared smile with lips that might as well have been pasted on. "Yes?" she says carefully, knowing that it's my voice summoning her: the all mighty messiah calling for her attention.

"I'd like an A on this."

"Sure, thing. We'll talk," she answers in a squeak.

In later classes, I raise my hand but my teachers pretend not to see it. Their eyes pass right by me, and they go on with their lecture. The only time that I can draw their attention is if I speak out on my own, uncalled. When that happens they try to appease to my request quickly and move on after holding their breaths for a long moment.

Finally, the last period of the day comes: American history. My excitement for the subject dropped when I first met our teacher, Mr.

Trouver. He talks in a slow, monotone voice that would put a speed addict to sleep. He elongates each word in a dull, jaw-extended sound of meshed syllables, making his voice come through nasal and stuffed.

"During World War II," he says with the entire class being quiet and our eyes drooping with boredom, "the women work force increased dramatically. Can anybody tell me why the level of women employment increased by so much?" He points to a chart drawn on the blackboard showing a scale increasing in percentage. Nobody ventures a guess. A few seconds pass and I decide to raise my hand. Mr. Trouver looks right past me.

"Well the answer is simple," he says. "A lot of men were at war, and the women were the only ones left to fill their jobs." I lower my hand. This is pointless. "Now," he says with the same lamenting voice, "you will be paired in groups of four and will work on this worksheet. You only need one sheet per group. I want it done by the end of class, today."

During Mr. Trouver's lecture, no one talks. No one farts, yawns, chews gum, taps his feet on the ground, or makes any other noises that might "disrupt" his class. He takes the fun right out of anything we do. He tolerates nothing, and would gladly send anyone to the office for doing anything as little as breathing too heavily.

He has us count off by seven. When my turn comes, I call out, "Three," and students get up from their seats to form their groups. I look around for my own group; they're probably hiding from me.

"Hey, Jeremy," a girl's voice says to me as I'm looking around. I turn and see a lean brunette standing in front of me with a hand on her round hip. She stands as if she were a Levi's model. Her firm legs are wrapped tightly by a pair of blue jeans. She's wearing a black, long-sleeved shirt with the word ANGEL written across the chest in silver letters. A light gold necklace hangs from her neck weighed down by a small golden cross. Her hair curls down to her cheeks in tight waves. She smiles down at me with full pink lips, shined over with gloss. A thin row of white teeth peeks out. Finally, my eyes find hers, and I find myself swimming in their immensity. They look as if whole acres of green prairie grass have been captured in them. I don't know what to say. A simple hi would be enough to respond to her "Hey, Jeremy," but my lips can't produce even that much.

"Is it true what it says in the papers?" she asks, still smiling. My lips widen to a grin. I sit back in my chair, and cock my head to the side.

"Are you in my group?" I say.

"No, I'm in group four. So, is it true?"

"Honestly, I don't even know. I fell asleep during what they claim happened."

She smirks at my answer, as if bracing herself in case I was only joking. We are talking to each other as if the topic were as normal as walking the dog. She lifts an eyebrow and looks at me oddly, still holding that appealing smile that holds back a whole river of laughter.

"Are you telling the truth?" she asks.

"I wouldn't lie to an angel." She scoffs playfullly. "You know," I pause, "you're the first person I saw today, other than my friend Ben, who isn't scared of me."

"Why should I be afraid of you? You're only human."

"Maybe we should spread the word."

Suddenly we're interrupted by Mr. Trouver's voice. "You two!" he snaps. "Get in your groups, and get to work!" I look at him and he looks away fretfully, grabbing a pen and doodling with it aimlessly at his desk. I turn back around to look at the girl, but she's gone.

I step towards my group and suddenly it gets quiet. I sit down. "Is this group three?" I ask. A couple of them nod, but they don't say anything. "What are we supposed to be doing?" I say, not really caring either way.

They hesitate, then a guy answers in a crackled voice, "We're on question number four. We have to answer it by looking at the chart." He points at a graph printed on the worksheet. I nod, pretending to care. They obviously don't need my help, nor want it, so I slide my chair back enough to make room for my feet.

A girl reads off the question and the rest of them share their thoughts. My mind is nowhere near the women's work force during World War II. I'm still thinking about the cute brunette I just met, and I realize I don't even know her name.

I look at the faces of my group members one by one. Their eyes are too busy to be looking at me, all staring at the same spot on the paper.

Fuck this.

I turn my head in search of the girl. I find her surrounded by three other students, huddled up in a corner. I get up and walk towards her.

I tap on her shoulder and I fix my face in an inviting smile. "Hey, I never got your name—"

"Sir!" Mr. Trouver's voice barks at me. I turn around, and see him standing in front of his desk with his shoulders slouched. "Sir, I thought I told you to stay in your group."

"I was just ask—"

"Sir!" He cuts me off. God, how I hate when he calls me that. He pronounces the word as if it had an "a" in the middle of it. If snails could talk, his voice is what they'd sound like. He flaps his hand at the wind, gesturing me to go back to my seat.

"Let me just ask her something," I plead with my lips curling back, and my eyebrows buckled down to the top of my nose. Somehow my voice still sounds more composed than I'd imagined it would.

"No, I think you best sit down." He closes in on me with narrowed, fixated eyes. He tries not to look away. He tries to look intimidating. In reality, I know he's more scared of me than I am supposed to be of him.

"Now listen to me, Mr. Trouver. You might choose to be the dull, crooked-smiled motherfucker that you are, but just because you choose to be boring, it doesn't give you the right to bring us down with you." I take a step closer to him and he backs up, stopping when cornered against the front of his desk. "What's wrong, Mr. Trouver?" I ask, still snarling through my teeth. His eyes are hazy with fear, searching for something— his own balls probably. "Are you afraid I'll fly up in the air and shit down on your face?"

He gulps hard, and I can see his Adam's apple pump up and down in his throat. His eyes widen in a shocked gape, and his mouth gasps a soundless gasp that I know must have pressed a lot of air through his lips. He goes back behind his desk and sits down at his chair like a scared poodle. Nobody talks. The entire room is so quiet that you can hear the uncomfortable seconds ticking past.

I go back to the girl and I find out her name is Jessica Davis.

Chapter 6

Walking out to the school parking lot, I shadow my eyes from the sun with one hand and begin my search for my car. Every day I forget where I parked it, and today is no different. Patches of snow cover the roofs of the cars, making it that much harder to find mine from the rest.

I step through a thick crowd of kids waiting for their bus, and just as earlier today, people make way. Then my shoulder bumps another, and I turn. Here I'm expecting to see the same frightened eyes of some pathetic, fretful, shit-faced kid who's going to run screaming, afraid he'll burst into flames, but I don't. These eyes I see before me are of a different slant in expression. They're not wide in an amazed awe or in any resemblance of fear, but instead they dart into my own.

A black lipstick-painted mouth speaks below those eyes. It says, "Move it, you fucking freak!" Each curve of the mouth's movement accents the dividing syllables in a disgusting, raspy voice.

The pale face is familiar. I recognize it, having seen it this morning. The guy's hair is dyed black and reaches out in all directions, like wild grass slicked in petroleum. A thin streak of black eyeliner outlines his eyes, surrounding those two black holes that peer out from his face. Those dark eyes are deep enough to fall into, and the pupils submerge into the blackness of their irises. The black lipstick covering his mouth extends outward like a tormented smile that reaches halfway up his cheeks. He wears a long trench coat that covers his arms down to his fingernails—which, too, are painted black—and goes down to the heels of his black combat boots. It seems that everything from head to toe is black on this idiotic Satan worshiper's body. The only white is his pale skin that barely shows, making an odd contrast against the rest of him.

Although his make-up makes him look like he's smiling, his firm, closed lips and his burrowing eyes tell a different story. He looks like a demented clown hired by the devil circus-master, unruly to even his own expression. And according to Gammy, that's exactly what Hell is: a huge chaotic circus where the only entertainment is your own torture.

"What'd you call me?" I ask firmly with a crooked stare. "Did *you* call *me* a freak? I'm not so sure you find the irony in that statement." I step closer to his artificial smile, but he doesn't back away. I didn't expect him to.

"You don't scare me," he tells me with the tip of his nose just above my own. Our eyes lock in a ballistic staring contest. "You think your weak God will reign this world for long? You're about to get something coming to you. These upcoming days of judgment, if there will be such a thing, will only provide for King Lucifer's victory. My Lord will show you. My Lord will show *Him*."

This nutcase has really popped off his hinges. He's a fucking crackerjack! He's not simply a morbid wannabe, he's a frickin' lunatic. This isn't what infuriates me, though. His comments about God aren't even close to what tempers my rage, considering I don't even believe in his existence. This kid assumes that he knows me. He called me a freak because he assumes he knows what in his far-fetched hell he's talking about. Assumptions can be dangerous, and I'm willing to show him exactly how dangerous they can be.

After this hellish day, all I wanted to do was go home, but now I find myself wanting to finish off a little errand before I go. The errand is to choke this little satanic freak's throat until his face, too, turns hued in black and maybe a bit blue as well. Then he'll be able to get a taste of Hell with his own swollen tongue and scorched tonsils.

"What's your name?" I ask the pale-faced moron, with all the coolness of the world coming out with my words.

He hesitates a moment, undecided of whether he should tell me or not, and then he does. "Tyler."

"Tyler what?"

"Crandall"

"Well, Crandall. Since you claim Satan is such a good friend of yours, maybe we can arrange a visit. What do you say?"

This black-on-white loon has no idea what's coming to him. In four years of high school, I've gotten myself in 27 fights from freshman year to senior. Ben had kept track of them, each one individually. He's like my secretary when it comes to this sort of thing, filling a small notebook with jotted notes ever since my first fight. Out of those twenty-seven I lost just one, which—in my defense—was against a huge black guy who weighed twice as much as me. I should've thought twice about smacking that two-by-four across his neck. He had fell with his knees locked and his fat rolling, but it wasn't an "out cold" kind of fall, which is what I had hoped for. Next thing I knew, his arms were around my head, crushing it like a walnut in a nut cracker. This lunatic, though, couldn't weigh more than a hundred and forty pounds with his trench coat on.

"Take your coat off," I tell him. "Looks expensive."

He scoffs.

"It might weigh you down," I go on. "I just want to give you a fair chance."

He lets the black coat flap heavily to the ground. The wind blows bitterly against his scrawny body as if to try and blow him away. Sometimes, I think that the cold is never going to go away. His white arms show now, and blue veins bulge out in streams from his wrists up his bamboo-thin arms. His black tee-shirt shows a wicked smiley face and below, in red letters, it reads: *THE ONLY WAY TO GET RID OF TEMPTATION IS TO GIVE INTO IT.*

Before I can finish reading the last line, he swings a tight ball of a fist at my face. The arched swing of his arm shows indeed that he is a stranger to fighting, tossed as if to pitch a baseball instead of a punch. I grab his swinging punch by the wrist and twist it in my grip.

In order to be a good fighter, you've got to acquire certain techniques. There is a certain style your body must assume to conquer or even survive a fight. Fighting is more than ballet or learning how to dance jazz. It isn't graceful, for one, and secondly, there isn't a beat that you can accommodate to. The only music you hear is that of grunts squirming brought to the lips of the defeated, accompanied by sweat and tears mixed on their pained mugs.

In a fight, not only do you need to think your way through it, but to do so quickly. The problem with most beginners isn't that they don't know *how* to fight, but that their minds freeze up at the first hint of panic, like the venom of a spider stiffening its pray. Their brains become blank, turning them into rag dolls instead of men confronting danger.

I've never fought anyone who falls under that category. It would take away the enjoyment from this bare-knuckled sport. There are other requirements that come along as well, though. If you're lucky enough to fight a worthy round, you must be able to know how to hit, where to hit, and when to hit. It's all in the timing. It's all in the endurance. But if you're not privileged with a fight with glamour, the most you'll do is roll on the ground, wrestling. Most of the time it comes to that.

I've fought guys who gave it their best in the first five minutes and then were too exhausted by the time I charged with my own attack. You can't expect to just swing blindly and be lucky enough to hit your opponent. Most people forget that their opponent doesn't *want* to get hit, and therefore he'll actually try to dodge those punches or kicks or whatever else that comes at them. Some people get into a fight and expect their opponent to actually stand still and take the beating.

I use this expectation to my advantage whenever it seems profitable. I dodge, and I dodge, and I dodge. It takes barely any effort to skip around while the other person swings away, sweating and cussing at you to keep still. I jump inches out of their reach just instants before they expect to make contact. In five minutes of chasing and swinging, a man can get pretty winded. And once that happens, it's my turn to counterattack.

For Tyler, though, I don't have five minutes of my time to waste on fight number twenty-eight. I just want to finish it off as quickly as possible and get to my car. So I twist tighter on his wrist in a counterclockwise turn, and he bends his torso to ease the pain. I yank him lower to the ground, and thrust my knee upward into his face.

He jerks backwards, but I yank him back again towards me, bringing his cheek into my other hard elbow. Blood trickles out of his nose in swirls. I'm proud to have added color to his face. He tilts back limply and I release my grip on his wrist, letting him fall to the ground.

He falls onto a pile of snow, sinking lifelessly into it. I don't bother with finishing him off. He's not moving either way, and if I kept hitting him, the only difference it would make is the time it would take him to recover. Students stand around us, looking back and forth from me to him. Two teachers assigned bus duty just stand there looking at me with their hands fingering a radio, unsure if they should use it to call someone.

Would a Messiah really resort to violence? Think about it. How can I be a messenger from God? But they just gape at me. In their minds I probably destroyed an evil demon from hell. I know better, though. He's just a kid lost in this world of deception.

I walk away.

What would my father think of me if he saw me right now? How I've let him down and his efforts to fill me with peace. I always think back to him when something like this happens. I can't even settle an argument without resorting to fists.

I remember coming home crying to my dad when I was still a little boy. This was back in third grade. One of the other kids had been picking on me, and had been pushing me around all day. That was the first time I remember having urges of violence. Can you believe it? I can still remember the very first time I felt hatred towards someone.

"Tomorrow, when you see him, share these with him," my dad said, taking out a handful of bite-sized chocolate bars wrapped in gold foil.

"A bribe?" I asked.

"No, a peace offering."

I didn't think it would work. I was so sure the boy would keep torturing me anyway. But he didn't. That boy was Ben Norton, and we've been best of friends since.

I just wish there was enough chocolate in the world to solve every problem.

Chapter 7

I park my car in an empty gravel lot just beyond a grass field behind my house. I keep the car this far from the house so that I can go out at night without having the rumble of my engine waking up Gammy. From here to my back yard, it's really only a two minute walk. I come in through the back, locking the door behind me.

Romulus greets me like he does every day. He wags his furry tail and stretches his lips back, smiling at me. "Did you feed Romulus?" I ask Gammy who's hunched over the kitchen table, sipping on a cup of coffee. She's wearing the same thin cotton robe she was this morning. If she hadn't switched chairs, I would've thought that she had sat at that table all day. She shakes her head no and says nothing. Scattered, tight wrinkles from her eyes, which are usually as gentle as ripples in pond water, slope downward at grievous angles.

I grab two cans from the cupboard, one in each hand, and face them, label-first, towards Romulus. "Which one is it going to be?" I ask, giving him the choice. He paws closer to me and licks my left hand, holding a can of Campbell's soup. "What a dumb doggy you are!" I tell him in the way people talk to pets. "Yes you are!"

I put the can of soup back in the cupboard and open up the other one instead. I dump the gooey, processed meat in his bowl and he starts munching at it.

"Did you hear the news, Gammy?"

"Hmm?" She doesn't look up from her fidgeting hands. The mug is now resting on the table between her arms.

"Did you hear I'm the new Christ? But of course you already knew that, didn't you? You were with me when it happened."

"Don't you say that! Don't you *ever* call yourself that again! Don't claim to be someone you are not. Your name is Jeremy, and just because

42

these journalists are too ignorant to recognize the difference between you and a Messiah, it doesn't give you the right to call yourself that." Her voice is angry and comes out crisply through her thin, wrinkled lips. Throughout the whole time she tells me this, our eyes never leave each other. She looks at me, swiping her eyes with a guilt-stricken stare.

"Gammy..." I say apologetically, looking for something to say, "I didn't mean to..." I'm at a loss for words.

"I know you didn't, honey, I know. And I'm sorry for yelling at you. It's just that a lot of people have been calling today wanting to talk to you. A lot of journalists were pressing me to schedule an appointment. I've just been really stressed out."

"What did you tell them?"

"I told them that there would be no appointment, and to leave you and me alone about the subject."

I'm glad she said that. She knows me well after all. But I'm still left with one question in mind that has been bothering me all day. I know that the only way I could believe any of this is if I asked her. "So is it true?" I force myself to ask, speaking softly through my unmoving lips.

She's silent, but I know she heard me.

"Is it really true that I..." how could I say it without actually saying it? "...that I flew? And that I said those things in front of everyone?"

I knew that whatever she'd say, I would believe it. Even if she told me, "No, honey. None of it is true," I would believe her. I would stand by whatever she'd tell me even if everybody else in the entire world told me differently. Unfortunately, I know already what the answer is going to be, but I need to hear it coming from her.

"Yes, Jeremy. It really *did* happen." She speaks almost as if she were sorry. I can detect the fear in her voice, and for the first time in nine years I feel scared beyond recognition. I'm scared of both this world and of my own self. The way she said it, too, was disturbing. She looked at me straight in the eyes, just like she always does when telling me something she needs me to understand, the way you'd understand beauty in nature or terror at night. And if I can't understand it, she expects me to at least accept it. She had looked at me that same way when she told me my parents were dead. I had seen their deaths with my very own eyes, and yet she had to tell me herself for it to finally sink in. Some people need to see to believe. But I guess that I don't believe until Gammy tells me it's true. Even then, though, there are still things I question.

My mind begins to rush. I sit down heavily, breathing in air that tastes contaminated with the mysteries of life suddenly brought into existence. Sitting down, I take in heavier and deeper breaths, always left disappointed by the taste of each one.

"Why me?" I ask, almost accusingly.

She hesitates to answer, swallowing before she speaks. "You don't know why God chose you, and neither do I. Only *He* knows why you were chosen. You have a good soul, Jeremy. You are a wonderful person even if you might not know it. Unfortunately, ever since Trevor and your mother died, you've gone astray in your decisions. God hates to see a good soul go to waste. Maybe *that* is why He's using you."

"Why *me*, though? There are six and a half billion people on Earth. Why did he get *me* to be his designated messenger? I'm sure there are more '*lost souls*' than just me!" I spoke that two-word pair mockingly.

"Because God loves us each individually. He cares about you just as much as he does for anyone else on this Earth. And He has found his own personal way to prove it to you. You have to accept His love into your heart, Jeremy. If only you had read the Book I bought you for Christmas, you would know all of this." The book she refers to is the Bible. I haven't touched it ever since I put it under the leg of my bed to sturdy it. "I use it everyday," I could tell her, but I don't think she would find the joke as amusing as I do.

"But don't think this is solely about you, Jeremy," she says, still holding my attention. "Obviously God has something big, maybe *huge*, planned ahead of us, and you're only a small part of it all."

The phone rings. Neither Gammy nor I budge at the sound. We look at each other for a second of silence. Then it rings again. I pick it up, and I speak softly, "Hello?"

"Hi, may I speak with Jeremy Christ?" The voice is upbeat and talks at a fast pace.

"That'd be me."

"Well, hello! This is Patrick West from the *New York Times*. I was wondering if we could schedule a meeting together. I'm free this weekend and could fly out to Detroit, lickety-split. I would greatly appreciate just an hour of your time…"

"Not interested," I say, and hang up the phone. Grandma looks at me understanding, and smiles approvingly.

Before I can turn around to go to my room, the phone rings again. I pick it up in my hand. A voice starts to talk before I can even say anything. "Hello, this is Claire Sanders from the *Pittsburgh Post Gazette*. I already called earlier this morning; is Jeremy Christ available?"

"Leave me alone," I say annoyed into the holes of my receiver, and slam it down hard. It rings again, and I bring the receiver to my ear again.

"Hello?" I snarl angrily with the tip of my tongue flicking at my teeth.

"Hey, Jeremy! It's Jessica, from school—"

"Quit calling me!" I scream. I'm about to slam the phone for a last time when I repeat the name in my head. *Jessica.* Feeling a little embarrassed, I put the phone back to my ear. "Sorry about that, I thought you were a journalist."

She laughs a broad, clear laugh as if she knew exactly what I was talking about. It made me feel good because I knew she wasn't offended.

"So, what's up?" she asks me. Her voice sounds jazzy and sexy over the phone.

"Nothing much. People have been calling all day wanting an interview."

"Wow, you're popular!"

"Yeah, but I wish I weren't. This is more of a pain in the ass than it is flattering. So, what's going on?"

"Oh, I just looked up your name in the school directory and decided to call you." I can sense a smile on her face as she is saying this. I love girls who take initiative. "You know, you really have some guts for telling Mr. Trouver off today."

"Well, somebody had to say something. All he does is boss us around. I think I got to him today."

There's a small pause of silence and then she asks me, "Are you scared?"

"No, I don't think he'll do anything about it. He was pretty embarrassed in class. I bet he won't even tell the principle."

"No, I mean, are you scared for when July comes?"

The question bothers me for a moment. "Now that you bring it up...a little. I haven't even thought about that part yet. I'm still dealing with the fact that I flew. When I threatened Mr. Trouver to fly right in front of him, I didn't believe it. It was an empty threat. A bluff. But he *did* believe it. I saw it in his eyes. He was scared of me, *truly* scared of me. And now I almost feel sorry for him."

"This morning," Jessica says, "I talked to my dad about, you know, the event that happened at your church. My friends call me pretty gullible because I believe just about anything I read on the news, so when I read the part about the judgment days I was freaked out. My dad seemed pretty troubled by the news, too. Like his face—I dunno, it was drained. I asked him what I'm supposed to expect, but he said he wasn't sure. He said that it could be pretty much anything, and that scared me even more. It's so much harder to deal with something when you don't know how to prepare for it."

"Well, I'm not really the person who can provide much comfort," I say. "I was the last one to find out about this little miracle, and I didn't even believe in it until I just talked to my grandma."

"What did she say?"

"Nothing that helped any," I say, making sure Gammy isn't listening, "She told me that God loves me and he has a reason for picking me. If anybody is going to pass this thing in July is going to be her. She's always reading the Bible, and praying to God." I try to say the last sentence with a sense of dismay, but instead it comes through sympathetic. This is the very first time I've mention God in a conversation with someone other than a family member. I'm surprised at how easily the words flow out. I don't even feel awkward talking about it. Maybe it's because she's the one who brought up the subject.

"And you?" she asks curiously.

"What about me?"

"Are you religious?"

"No, not at all. And I'm probably more scared than you are because I'm so confused. It's easy to believe something when it's not happening to you. It's easier to deal with it when it's happening to someone else, but I'm right smack in the middle of it. I didn't even believe in God at all, and then *this* happened. It's really making me question my non-faith." I laugh quietly to myself at the dry joke. Jessica does too, amused, cheering me up a bit.

"So you believe in God now?"

"I…I guess I'll have to."

"My advice would be to ask your grandma for help. I'm glad I called you."

"Why's that?"

"Because if *you're* scared then I guess it's okay for me to be. Well, I've got a lot of things to do, so I better get going. I'll see you tomorrow, Jeremy."

"Looking forward to it, Jessica."

I put down the receiver. I'm not surprised when I hear it squeals again right into my hand. I sigh deeply, and decide not to pick it up.

"Who was that?" Gammy asks curiously.

"Jessica. A girl I met today at school."

"Is she a nice girl?"

"She seems like it."

"Well, good. I'm going to take a shower. When I get out I'll make us some dinner."

"It's not even three yet."

"It'll be a long time before I get out," she says, smiling tiredly.

She must have had a tough day. She normally takes her showers first thing in the morning. Inside the shower is the only place in this house where you can relax for as long as you want. You can zone out without worries, isolated from everything by the sound of the water rushing down on your face. I almost feel like a shower myself.

Instead I walk to our answering machine. I wonder how many of those phone calls Gammy didn't even bother picking up. The small red digits are flashing. The number reads fifty-seven new massages. I don't even bother.

I look at the counter, looking for college mail advertising to me, convincing me that they're the best university to go for. But looking at the counter today I don't see any of the fliers I usually receive. Gammy must have forgotten to check the mailbox. The phone keeps ringing, and I ignore it. Then the answering machine beeps, and a few seconds later a new number flashes on the digital display. I walk outside, heading towards the mail, but I stop dead at the doorsteps, shocked by what I see.

Chapter 8

There must have been at least a hundred of them on my front lawn, all grouped together as if to keep each other warm in the cold weather. As soon I step out, they begin chattering incoherently, throwing their loud voices and pointing their microphones at me. Even the street is entirely lined with news vans from every possible TV station that you can think of.

I turn around, trying to go back inside, but the doorknob won't turn. It just wiggles tightly, and I know I locked myself out. I turn back to the crowd with my back pressed against the door and decide that I might as well get the mail after all. I take weary steps down the porch, which creaks stiffly at my weight. They all swarm towards me.

For a long time now I've realized that reporters aren't people who believe in much of anything. They're here not because they think that I'm a messenger from God, but because this could be the biggest story of the century, and if they stand here in the cold asking their stupid little questions, it's bound to pay off. They want to know, "Who are you?", "Why are you so important?" and "How can you make *me* some good money?" And actually, it might pay off even more if they succeed in twisting my words around to make me say whatever they want to hear, instead. So as I walk past them, they don't back away like the scared students of West Bloomfield High. Rather, they press against me, shoving their microphones in my face like force-feeding ice cream cones to a diabetic.

"What can we expect of these so called 'Judgment Days'?" a lady with blonde hair asks, wasting no time at all. She pierces through the word "judgment" with a tone of scoffing skepticism. I keep shouldering my way through as if being surrounded by five to six feet of snow. I wave my arms in arches, swimming through the crowd, pushing people to the sides.

"Nothing!" I answer her as I keep pushing forward. "Leave me alone."

"So you are denying that the 'Judgement Days' will have any effect on us?" the same lady presses, beginning the first act of word-twisting of this already uncomfortable interview. The entire crowd moves along with me, making it harder for me to reach the mailbox. Why did I even bother?

"I'm not saying anything. Just let me through."

"Is it true that you got in a fist fight this morning at school?" a pudgy man in glasses asks from behind me. I look at him just long enough to see his chubby cheeks blubber as he talks.

I keep pressing with my legs, barely gaining any advantage in distance. "It wasn't this morning," I tell him, "it was after school."

"Shouldn't you, as a Messiah, act peacefully and lovingly in accordance with others?"

I could easily be just a few feet away from the mailbox (which I can't see because of the crowd), but it still would be a few impossible feet too many. With each step I take I get pushed back two more. I'm surrounded by a sea of heads and shoulders that won't leave me alone and just won't let me get the fucking mail!

"I'm not a Messiah!" I scream into his face, which has somehow moved in front of me. How the hell can these people move so swiftly in this chaotic mess, when I wouldn't even be able to pick a wedgy if I had to? The answer, of course, is simple. They're reporters, and they're used to this. They slick and slide just like leeches do to grab a hold of whatever blood they're after.

"So, are you saying that none of the prophetic events will happen?" some other person shouts.

"I'm just saying I'm not a Messiah. Okay? Quit putting words in my mouth, and let me…" I grunt as I'm swayed right back by my torso, "…get to my mailbox!"

But they won't budge. They just keep poking me in the face with their damned microphones, making soft patted thuds as they hit me in the nose or on the cheek. I grab one from a reporter's grip and throw it on the street where it clunks, hopefully breaking to pieces. "Hey!" the man yells at me.

"'Hey' nothing!" I justify, poking a flat fingertip at his chest. "Now I'm not going to answer *any* more questions until I get my mail! All right?" As soon as I scream this, people spread out.

"Excuse me," I say as I nudge a few remaining reporters to the sides with my elbows. I don't even know where the mailbox is, but I look around. All I know is that it's hidden somewhere among these people. Finally I see a metal edge of it sticking out from behind a man. I head towards it, and they just watch me walk past them.

I step in front of the box and I grab the little tab. The metal is dented inward from people pushing and pressing against it. I have to yank at the door with both hands to force it open.

I look inside. Other than its own indents, the metal box is completely empty. I made the trip out here for nothing! With the mailbox opened, the questions rush in all at once, making very little sense.

I hear someone scream, "Jeremy, what should people Jesus new man messiah potato chip?" and I figure that must have been about fifteen different voices blended in together. Hearing this, I slam the metal box shut. I grab it by its base and I rattle it furiously. The metal pole stings my hands with its cold surface. I keep rattling it and more questions swarm in. My fingers go numb and my knuckles stiffen up from the cold.

The same woman from before asks, "What's in the mail box, Jeremy?"

What the hell do you think is in the mailbox, lady? I want to yell at her. *It's empty! It's fucking empty, and for whatever reason I feel better if I rattle the living shit out of it, imagining it was one of you I was choking by the neck! Okay? That's what's in it! Nothing!*

I groan angrily, breathing out a warm puff of air. Then I'm shaking the base so violently that the top—which had already come loose at the hinges—falls off, falling to the snow on the ground. I don't stop. I keep vibrating the pole like a jackhammer, widening the hole in the ground, making the pole looser and looser. I yank at the pole hard with another tug, and it rips out of the ground and goes flying in helicopter spins out of my grip. Instinctively, people duck, barely missing the pole's spin that could've slammed into their heads. A few reporters trip backwards, falling on the ones behind them, and consequently they tumble like human dominoes. They're distracted.

I run.

I trip over a reporter who's struggling on the ground, making me fall to my hands and knees. I fight to crawl away from the jumbled mess of people, but finally slip away. Behind me, the domino effect is just coming to an end. Men and women are on the ground, pulling on each other to help themselves up.

In a few doggy steps I trod onto my walkway and get up to my feet. Slowly the reporters regain balance.

They scream after me.

I squeeze between my house and my neighbor's. The two houses are separated by a gap slightly wider than my shoulders' width. The walls are so close that they feel like they are slowly closing in on me to crush my body. I manage to slip all the way out and hop over my backyard fence. My foot catches on the top link and I trip, smacking chest-first against the ground.

The thud leaves me breathless and lightheaded. My pant leg tugs at the top of the fence, and I can't get it free. I wiggle my foot, trying to get it loose but only manage to rip a hole through the cuff of my pant leg.

A few of the reporters start fighting like kids shoving for their personal space, struggling with each other in the gap. The pudgy man from before gets stuck, blocking the others' path. Angry, the others push him from behind, and Pudgy's love handles scrape against the two walls. Men and women scream at him to budge, and he screams back at them in pain.

I pull my foot free from the fence and struggle back to my feet. The story-hungry journalists walk on the pudgy man, stepping on him like a bridge. I run to the back door, but of course it's locked. More and more reporters get stuck in the tight gap, clogging it like a drain. Only some manage to get through. A woman gets her head yanked backwards by the hair by another female reporter who struggles to get to me first. The two women begin to catfight in the pathway, stopping anyone else from advancing. Blocked reporters squirm and scream, elbowing each other in the face, kneeing one another in the gut, and doing anything they can to get passed the jammed walls.

I grab a large thermometer hanging from the wall, and turn it around in my palm. I open the little secret slot on the back of it to reveal the hidden key. I pinch fingers around it, but my hands are shaking so badly that I can't even keep a steady grip on the key. I look back and see the two women getting pushed hard out of the gap, like a cork popping from the mouth of a champagne bottle. The reporters flow through, one after the other, stepping on anyone else who stands in their way.

In the middle of my fidgeting with the key, I pause to see the two women ripping clothes off each other. The blonde reporter's bra is showing and for a moment I stare, forgetting what my initial purpose for coming back here was. Their little show is almost worth getting attacked by a hungry pack of reporters. The two squirming women get pressed against the metal linked fence and get used as footsteps by their rivals.

Two men climb over the fence and one falls, tripping just the way I did, with a foot caught on the fence. He grabs the other man by the ankle, and he too flops to the ground, getting a taste of dirt and snow mixed in together.

My hand shakes as I try to push the key into its hole. The key's little teeth bite at the sides of the knob, missing the slot. I squat down, bending my knees, bringing myself at an eye-level with the sliver hole. I stick my tongue out, pressed tightly between my lips, as if to help me concentrate. I surround the knob in a fist with my free hand and stab it with the key. I poke at it a few more times, each missing, and then finally it slides smoothly in. I turn, push, and the door swings open.

A couple of the reporters are just a few feet behind. In panic I run inside, almost tripping over myself. I slam the door behind me and lock it, forgetting that the key is still in the hole outside. The scrambling buffoons approach closer to the door with clothes torn, wrinkled, and even missing. I open the door quickly to reach my hand through and yank out the key. I slam the door again and lock it.

I'm hunched over, panting hard, with one hand to my knee trying to support my weight, and the other hand holding the key to my chest. The warm air inside the house helps me regain feeling in my frozen hands. My lungs expand and compress. Through the key I can feel my heart pounding furiously. The pounding is so strong that it feels like my heart is going to explode with a plop in my chest.

My mind is fogged and everything feels light, all the excess blood rushing through my temples. I sit on the floor with my knees pointing up and my legs spread, hoping that the rapid beating subsides, but now it's coming on so heavily that it feels like the entire house is shaking. The windows rattle. The door bursts in continuous attacks. I realize then that it's not my heart doing all this, but the reporters outside banging at the door and walls.

I lean my back against the door and let its rattle massage my shoulders. My muscles relax. It feels…oh, so good.

Gammy comes out of her bathroom wrapped in a light blue bathrobe. Her slippers swish-swoosh on the ground. She pinches up her robe with one hand so it won't drag against the floor. "What in the heck is all that noise?" she asks, a bit shaken.

I keep my eyes closed, enjoying the soothing vibration on my back. "We're being invaded by reporters; take cover!" I say. My words come out in vibrated syllables sounding as if spoken into a spinning fan.

She looks out the window. "Oh dear!" she exclaims. "There's so many of them!" She slides the glass window up, and sticks her torso out, keeping her hands on the windowsill for leverage. Although muffled by the walls, I hear her yell, "Please get away from my house, and off my property!" They ignore her. Instead of leaving, they shout their voices and blabber questions incoherently.

"No comment."

More questions and shouting.

"I have nothing to say!"

She gives up and just closes the window gently.

"Jeremy!" Gammy says to me. "Is it true you tried to hit a reporter with the mail box pole?" She looks concerned.

"Gammy, come here and put your back against this door. You gotta feel this."

She paces over and looks down at me. She's still pinching her robe with a thumb and forefinger. "What did you do?"

"Nothing," I say. "I went outside to get the mail, and saw all those people on our front lawn. The mailbox was all beat up. When I found out that there was no mail, I started shaking the mailbox…" I gesture with both hands the universal signal of choking someone by the neck. "Then before I knew it, the thing slipped out of my hands and went flying. It didn't hit anyone, but came pretty close."

The way I said "slipped" sounded ridiculous. It sounded like I was telling the story only at a half-truth level so to cover something up. But that's exactly what happened. It slipped. Didn't it?

The door stops shaking. Gammy looks down at me in skepticism. She doesn't buy it. It seems that the only time I tell the truth, others think I'm lying. Suddenly, I don't really believe it myself either.

I try to think back to exactly what happened.

I picture myself holding the pole in my hands. I see it shooting out, faster than I've ever seen anything move. *Did* I throw it intentionally?

No. That's crazy. It was just an accident. I didn't even try to yank it out of the ground, but that's exactly what happened.

Then I think of the massive speed the pole moved once it was airborne. I couldn't possibly have thrown anything that fast. I'm not nearly *that* strong. It just spun furiously through the air, and yet it didn't hit anyone. Everyone was able to duck just in time before they'd be left with a gash across the face or, worse yet, decapitated. All of it felt too weird. Too...unreal.

Then there was that *other* thing.

Pulling the pole out of the ground sounds pretty farfetched at first. It would require a hell of a lot of strength to do it, especially considering that the ground is frozen stiff, but maybe an adrenaline rush can justify it. People have been known to accomplish extraordinary feats of strength during moments of panic or excitement. So I guess that explains the fury in its launch, but what about the shiver of shock I felt?

Right before the metal pole ripped out of the ground, I felt a bolt of electricity start at the tip of my fingers, making them twitch. It felt like hooking up two ends of a jumper cable to a car battery, and the other two right to the palm of my hands. Not that I've ever done that, but I figure. The shock flowed up my arms, through my chest and down to my feet.

Did I imagine it?

I've never had an adrenaline rush before, but I don't think they come with a spasm of electricity. The more I think about it, the less I believe that it was just my imagination playing a trick on me.

Could it have been an act of God?

HOPE

Chapter 9

About a month has passed since "the event," and we're now in middle of May. Most people refer to what happened as just that, "The Event." They don't know what *else* to call it. It's like giving a name to a new species, one that goes against the rules of nature and science. It's like calling that species "the thing" just like in that horror movie because you don't know what else to name it.

The Vatican in Rome decided to label it "Il Risveglio," which means "The Awakening" once translated in English. They say that the event has awakened hundreds of millions of Christians around the world back to worship the way it was always meant to be. Those who were once Christian, but not practicing Christians, finally began to reform themselves to the right ways of living. This is all according to studies and research that the Vatican has dwelled itself extensively into.

According to a research made by *Time* magazine, over twenty-three million Americans have converted to Christianity. The number of Church-going Christians in the United States has never been so high. People have been simply scared into praise.

I'm not on the list among those who have converted. Well, technically I was already a Christian before anything ever happened, but the life of worship is not for me. If what's going to happen is for real, then that means I have only a month and a half left to enjoy living before July, and I'm not going to do that by wasting my time praying.

For the past four Sundays, I refused to go to Mass with Gammy. She didn't like it, and every time we argued about it, but in the end she'd always leave the house without me. I just can't go back..

I need to have my fun, after all. If my life has to end at the age of 18, I might as well die knowing that it was all worth it. There are too many things I'll never get to extract out of life. Maybe getting married and have a bunch of rascals could have been part of it, who knows. That's not even a possibility anymore. I just need to let loose. I need to party and explore my own trapped world of Detroit. I haven't even gotten to know Jessica yet, and I better do something about it because time's running out. What can you do in the last month and a half of your life? How do you make it worth it?

I feel like I've been living in distraction all this time.

And if people weren't convinced that the world is coming to an end by "The Event," then the strange events that followed have made sure to do just that. The temperatures of May dropped to digits even more absurd than those of April. At first everyone was convinced that the cold weather was just a prolonged winter, and they had no doubt that it would pass by the end of April. But they were wrong.

The coldest recorded temperature in April was -12 degrees Fahrenheit. Just yesterday the temperature dropped to negative twenty degrees. The weekly forecast predicts that it will continue to decrease at a deathly rate. They can't say when spring is finally going to arrive. All they *can* say is that they're getting "peculiar" numbers that can't possibly be accurate. According to their computers and satellites, by the end of the month of May, temperatures will touch down to an impressive negative thirty-two, or even lower.

Despite the dangerous cold weather, there hasn't been a single account of homeless death. There are over six hundred homeless men and women living in the downtown streets of Detroit alone, and not a single one of them has had health problems due to the subzero temperatures. They should have all frozen to death by now, but miraculously they haven't.

A group of scientists decided to take in three of these homeless men for studies, using them like guinea pigs. The studies came through useless, though. All they found out was that the men were in a state of malnutrition and bad health due to reasons irrelevant to weather. Well, no shit! I could've told you that by just looking at them. I saw a picture of the three men smiling their gnarled grins in the article they published. They looked famished to the point where you could toss them a stripped-down bone, and they would probably jump to it like hungry dogs. Naturally, the scientists didn't try to convince us that the only way to survive the cold is to eat garbage from the dumpsters and visit the local soup kitchens. Those were the routines of the three homeless men, but it's doubtful that they would work for anyone else.

The weirdest thing about all of this is that the sky has never been brighter than in these days. Every day, the streets are illuminated by the brightest sun that has ever shone in the sky. It's impossible to be outside without shading my eyes to prevent from going blind. During the day, the sun shines so brightly that it pierces through my closed eyelids. And yet it doesn't emit any warmth. It's a fluorescent light bulb in the sky that has run out of heat.

It seems larger too. Well, it *feels* larger, is what I meant to say. Any fool who looks directly at this new sun and tells you it's gotten bigger deserves to go blind in the aftermath.

Again, more scientists—this time astrologers who have nothing better to do than to look up at the stars—have gone into studying this oddity. After two weeks of research and calculations, they declared that the flaming ball of fire has increased in volume by 40% compared to its original size. I'm not sure if these digits were rounded or if that was the exact volume increase the astrologers came up with. These are people without lives, if you ask me. In the end the scientists declared that instead of its original 1.392 billion kilometer diameter, the sun's width is now 1.9488 billion kilometers.

Despite this huge sun, it's still going to be the longest winter ever encountered in the United States. And it's not just up here in Detroit and in the Northern states where longer winters are a casual event. All of the 48 regional states are receiving snow, including the deep southern ones that have never seen a flake in their lives. Plus, the cold has spread to South America, Western Europe, East Asia, Northern and Central Africa, and even to countries in the Middle East. These places have been receiving snow since the end of April, which is when the coldest temperature of that month occurred up here, and it hasn't stopped snowing since. Schools and offices had to shut down, spreading from south Arizona to Alabama.

Schools have been closed for almost two weeks here in Detroit, which has given me a nice break from the unusual and unwanted attention. Students and teachers had finally begun to act differently towards me around mid-April and began to calm down. Some remained skeptical, but most others started to approach me with respect.

The members of the Fellowship of Christian Athletes, also known as FCA, began to approach me every day for guidance. They would press against me in the hallways, grasping onto my shirt, begging me to help them in their prayers and worries. So many would admit how they were losing their faith before "The Event," and I wanted to scream about how I've been losing my sanity since. But I said nothing. I tried to listen instead, not knowing what to tell them.

I felt like I was becoming one of those loonies on TV who calls people from the audience to heal them. To them I was one of those preachers who jabs a crippled man in the eyes, and miraculously he can stand up and tap dance to the cha-cha.

They all wanted me to do something, but what could I do for them? Should I have smacked my hand upon their foreheads and screamed, "Jesus Lord all Mighty! May your soul be healed and worry free. May your spirit fly with the birds and shit down on the hoods of cars!" I don't think so. That's just not my thing. At first all they wanted to do was to stay away from me. Now all they want is to be touched. To be saved. To be healed.

I tried to tell them that I'm not who they think I am, but the more I denied it, the more they wanted it to be true. They think I'm their savior. They think that I'm their miraculous Messiah who has been chosen to do something on this Earth.

I believe that I'm just a kid. Nothing more.

The last of the reporters had finally given up on me for an interview by the end of April. When the temperature began to decrease drastically, fewer and fewer reporters showed up on the front lawn with their microphones shivering in their gloved hands. Eventually they decided that getting an interview with me was not worth the frostbitten fingertips and lips so chapped that they would fall off with the first question they'd ask

Instead, just as I predicted they would, they each invented their own side of the story. According to reporter Jack Lester, from the *Free Press* news report, I'm a distant descendant of Jesus. Pretty unoriginal considering that the idea has already been thought of in the movie *Dogma*. To Cathleen Manning from the *New York Times* I'm a Moses-type leader with supernatural powers. She made me out to be some sort of religious superhero, fighting demons and eating Eucharist just in time before the end of the world. I wrote her a letter saying that Superman never had it this good. To so many others I'm the Antichrist, brought down to this Earth to destroy humanity. Each of the reporters came up with his or her own theory, and every reader pretty much believes whichever they read first. They all either love me or hate me. There isn't much of a middle ground for people to stand on.

But to Grandma, I'm just Jeremy Christ, and that's who I am to me.

Chapter 10

A large mug with a picture of a snowman on the front rotates awkwardly inside the microwave. Round and round it goes as little microscopic waves bounce off the side walls in every direction, increasing the friction of the water molecules in the mug.

The timer counts down. It stops at zero and then beeps twice. I push the large rectangular button, and the microwave's door pops open in an arched swing. I grab the mug by the handle with two fingers and a thumb and hold it out in front of me. The water bubbles a couple times, and heavy steam dances in curves, hovering atop it. I set it down on the counter and rip open a package of chocolate powder. The chocolatey dust pours down into the water and dissolves. I stir the mixture with a teaspoon until the powder is completely absorbed into the water. I add a few mini-marshmallows for the extra taste.

Pressing my lips against the edge of the mug, I tilt it in my hands slowly until the liquid barely touches my lips. Sipping slowly, I get a scent of what hot tastes like. To cool it down, I blow gently into the mug. The liquid ripples delicately at my blows, and I try to sip again. This time the rich taste of chocolate seeps onto my tongue, but it's still blended with the feeling of scalding iron.

The marshmallows turn into little white blobs floating on top of the brown liquid. One blob flows into my mouth, tasting milky and creamy. My cheeks tingle at the sensation of pleasure.

"How is it?" Gammy asks, not looking at me but out the foggy window.

"Pretty sweet. You want some?" I hold the mug out at her, in a gesture of offering. She turns to me and smiles.

"No thanks," she tells me, "I can't handle hot chocolate."

"How bad is it snowing out?"

"Pretty bad," she says with her smile softening a little.

"School's been closed for over two weeks. How much longer is it going to go on for?"

"The weatherman says it might go on all month."

"What do *you* say?" What the weatherman thinks doesn't mean shit to me.

"Well..." she hesitates, "I think it's going to keep going until July."

"July?" I say shocked, but still not very surprised. This weather, I'm sure, is no coincidence.

I'm a little annoyed by the cold. My nose has been redder than a drunk's and been dripping liquid for weeks, non-stop. Winter is not my favorite time of the year, and the fact that it's been going on for a month longer than what's considered normal is only giving me cringes of annoyance.

"Look, Jeremy, I'm sorry to have to ask you this..."

I look up at her from my warm mug.

"...but could you get the mail? It's been three days since we checked if we got anything." In the past three days we haven't left the house except to shovel the stone walkway, dump salt on it, or make quick runs to the store. I haven't even walked Romulus in a while. I just let him out mainly, knowing that he'll do his business quickly and come right back. I doubt that there's even going to be any mail at all. If I was a mailman, I'd quit my job.

"Sure." I smile brilliantly at her. I take a deep chug of the hot chocolate and grimace hard at the heat. It goes down my throat, leaving me with a slightly scathed tongue.

I set the mug back down on the counter to let it cool down.

Before even daring to step outside I layer myself with enough clothes that would put an Eskimo to shame. I walk to the main entrance closet and look through the jackets and coats. I spread hangers apart, trying to see better between the coats. As I slide them aside, I find my heavy gray coat and put it on. First I zip it from bottom to top and then I snap all the buttons closed. I slip my hands and fingers into thick gloves, and pull a black tussle cap that smells like wood fire smoke down over my head, covering the tip of my ears.

I step out and a gust of wind takes me by surprise. Forcefully, I close the door behind me, and the hinges squeak a bit. My breaths condense into visible warm clouds and then fade into the air. I step down to the walkway. To each side of me there is a wall of snow about four or five feet high. Little flakes continue to swoop down fast like jumpers without parachutes.

The walkway is frosted over with little crystals, forming a thin layer over the cracked stones. I plant my steps carefully, prepared for any ice that may be hidden somewhere.

We've changed the mailbox since the day of the journalists' invasion, replacing it with an all-wooden one. Long icicles drip down from the mailbox, frosting over the front and jamming the little door shut. I scrape at it with my fingers, but my gloves make the job impossible. My grip slips, barely scratching at the surface of the layered ice.

I pull the little tab but the door doesn't open. It's jammed. I reach in my coat pocket where I keep everything, and after a few seconds of fumbling for what I'm looking for, I grab a little Swiss army knife in my palm. Struggling with my gigantic padded fingers, I try to pull on the flappable blades. After a few failed tries I use my teeth to flip the biggest blade open, and I start picking at the ice with little jagged stabs. The knife crunches away the ice in little slivers, and after a few more stabs I manage to scrape the door free.

I look inside and find it packed with envelopes from top to bottom and from left to right. It's jammed so tightly that I have to take letters out one by one before I can loosen their grip on the inside walls. Looking through the envelopes I notice that the same name keeps repeating itself on practically all of the letters.

Except for two of them, they are all addressed to me.

I'm about to walk back towards the house when I notice three holes in the snow. They're too big to be footsteps, and nobody would be able to walk in four-feet-high snow and leave behind just three grooves where their legs stepped in.

I look down into the first hole and see a plastic shopping bag at the bottom. I reach in with my arm and pull the bag up, weighing heavier than I expected.

Inside of it are even more letters. Through the plastic I can make out a name on a few of them. They're all for me. I hunch over the other two holes and see the same type of plastic bag filled with letters at the bottom of each.

I shove the envelopes I got from the mailbox into several of my large coat pockets and pick up the three bags, carrying everything inside.

The warmth from inside the house rushes to my cheeks, grazing them like the soft touch of a mother. My ears feel hot and throb with the pumping of blood. I scrape the bottom of my shoes on the entering mat, and at the same time throw the bags at the couch in the living room. They thud heavily against the cushions.

"What's all this?" Gammy asks, looking at the invaded couch.

"The mail," I answer. I take off my hat and pull my gloves off. I throw it all in the closet not caring where it lands. I unzip my coat and walk into the living room, making sure that my shoes are well brushed off.

"That's a *lot* of mail. Is it bills?" she asks, her voice sounding worried over the possibility of being surrounded by bills.

I laugh a bit amused. "I hope not. Almost all of them are for me. There's more, too." I pull the rest of the letters out of my various pockets and start tossing them like playing cards on the floor. I pull out the last two envelopes, the ones addressed to Katherine E. Christ, and I hand them to her. She takes her two but doesn't stop looking at the rest. She doesn't even acknowledge the ones I handed her.

"What *is* all of this then?"

"I don't know, but I guess I'll find out."

Chapter 11

All of the letters were a cry for help. It took me an hour just to read all the ones I found inside the mailbox and most of the ones in the first plastic bag. I didn't stop reading even though after a while I realized that they were all asking for the same thing. The pattern became obvious, and I could predict almost each one before even opening it.

Most of those who wrote me included his or her own picture of a small baby, family members, or of themselves. Attached to some of the pictures there's a note simply saying, "Pray for us." I guess they think that if I can see what they look like it would make it easier for me to pray for them. Other letters are much lengthier than that. Some are anywhere between three to four pages long. The long ones each tell a story about the struggle that that specific family is going through. No shit, me too. Yet they all ask for *me* to do something about it!

What can *I* do?

They all call to me, pleading for a prayer or some sort of blessing. If I prayed for each and every person who sent me a letter I wouldn't even be finished by the time July rolled around. Do they realize what they're asking of me? Others tell me that they trust in me to guide them through this hardship.

Some of them are duplicates or repetitive letters sent by the same person who is afraid I didn't receive their first one, or their second, or their third. There's a man from Philadelphia who wrote six times, and that's just in the first pile. I'm sure I'll see more from him in the other two.

There's mail sent from all over the United States, at least one letter from each state. Plus there are others from Canada, Mexico, South America, Europe, parts of Africa, Japan, and countries in Asia where Christianity is practiced. Most of the ones from around the world speak

English pretty badly, making simple grammatical mistakes or spelling errors. Some of them are so incomprehensible that I had to quit reading after the first few lines. Others didn't even bother to speak English at all; they decided to write in their own language instead, assuming that I'd understand German, or French, or Japanese or whatever.

All the ones written in a foreign language sent pictures, apparently asking for prayers for their family. After I was done with the first plastic bag I grabbed four empty shoeboxes and filled them with pictures. One of them holds only pictures of cute girls or hot women. I know, I know, that's probably not right on my part, but those pictures are the only ones I'm interested in.

Some of the envelopes bulge up thickly. When I open those, I find some sort of trinket inside, sort of like a toy prize inside a cereal box.

People have sent rosaries, small golden crosses, medallions with a picture of a woman on the front, little framed pictures of a mother and a father holding a small baby, or jewelry such as silver rings or thin bracelets. They're all religious items, I suppose, even the ones I don't recognize. I'm pretty positive that the design of the man and woman holding a baby in their arms is about baby Jesus and his parents. Anybody would have been able to tell you that much. Although, I'll be damned to know what the names of both parents are. Mary and Abraham is my guess if you were to ask me, but I know that doesn't sound right.

The rings have words chiseled on them such as WWJD (What Would Jesus Do?) or chapters from the Bible. One of them reads ITHES 4: 3-4. The bracelets have a small cross or some type of charm attached to them. I kept all the items in a separate shoebox, making five boxes all together.

Gammy walks by and stops to look through the pictures and little trinkets. "Wow," she says. "They're really reaching out to you."

"Either that or they like to give away free stuff," I laugh, half amused.

"This isn't just stuff, Jeremy," she says coolly, helping me understand. "These are people's souls and beliefs. All these pieces of jewelry hold the Lord's blessing. They are giving you these blessings so you will give them back some of yours in return."

"I don't have anything to give them. How can I send jewelry to all these people?"

"They're not asking for materialistic objects. They're simply asking for your prayers. They know that if *you* ask God on their behalf, their wishes will be answered."

I don't know what she means by that. I don't think we're dealing with some sort of genie in a lamp here.

"What do they want me to pray about?" I ask.

"For God's guidance and protection through you. They understand that you represent a strong centerpiece on this Earth now, and that you're actually capable of accomplishing things."

"Pray for them?" I ask flatly, as if to suggest that there must be more to it than that. Where's the catch?

"Yes!" she says, sounding so near to excitement. Maybe she thinks that any of this is actually getting through to me, but little does she know that it's not. Truth is, I don't even know *how* to pray.

"How can I do that, Gammy? How can they possibly ask that of me? I don't even pray for myself, so how can I do it for them? Don't you see how many there are? There's at least two hundred letters in each bag!"

"Don't be so selfish," she says in a hushed calm, trying to reason with me.

"No, Grandma! I didn't ask for any of this I shouldn't have to pray for these people. They're not my responsibility. They're asking for charity from me. They're asking for something I'm not willing nor able to give them."

"Of course you can give it to them! They're not asking for much."

Our tones begin to heat up in our excitement. She's tries to keep her voice even-toned, but a few words slipped to reveal the tension of our conflict. Each of us tries to argue our point to the other—both of us fail miserably.

"You don't know that, Gammy. I can't give them what they're asking for. I just can't, all right?"

"You're being stubborn. This may be your chance to express your leadership through this blessing God has given you."

"Blessing? Blessing! Is that what you call it? Look outside, Gammy. Do you call *that* much snow a *blessing*? I call it a fucking catastrophe. I don't see any good coming out of this."

She gives me a harsh look, but I think it's more for mocking what she said than for swearing.

"What you see outside is only the beginning of what's ahead of us. If you refuse to pray for these people then *I* will. But you're going to send all the pictures and pieces of jewelry back."

I look at the five boxes full of pictures and shiny objects. I hold two of the boxes out to her. "Look at all of this! It's going to cost me more than I've got to send everything back! Besides, I don't even remember who sent me what."

"Well you better start remembering," she tells me, "because I'm not going to let you keep any of it."

I don't think she realizes what she's asking of me. I have neither the time nor the patience to play the matching game. There are over two hundred opened envelopes dispersed among the floor, and almost all of them contained something when I looked inside, whether a picture or a piece of jewelry. Some even sent more than one item. There is no possible way for me to figure this out. It would take me all night just to *guess* half of them.

She means it though. Her eyes, although they've cooled, offer a stern request without any other option or choice.

I start shuffling my hands through the opened letters, trying to see if any of them seem familiar. Gammy shuffles her feet out of the living room. Then I see one that strikes my attention, not because I remember what it's matched up to, because of the opposite.

I don't remember seeing this letter at all before. And yet I must have opened it.

The paper used for the letter is a three hole-punched, lined notebook paper. The writing on it is choppy, written in blue crayon. It looks like the handwriting of an elementary student. Attached to the back, with a paperclip, is a picture of a small boy holding up a baby girl in his arms with his two parents standing on each side of him.

I can tell the baby is a girl because she's wrapped up in a pink blanket. The boy doesn't look much older than seven. Both his mother and father have brilliant faces with radiant smiles that shine from cheek to cheek. The picture could be enlarged and easily used as a "Family of the Year" poster.

The words are written with a blue crayon, forming a series of scribbled letters.

Hi Jeremy,

My name is Benjamin and I'm seven and a half. I wrote because my aunt and uncle Margaret and Roy told me you can help. They said that you flied in the air and that you are a mirracle worker. I think you're an angel but they say that's not true. My mommy and daddy in the picture died in a car accident last month. I know that you can't make them come back to Earth from Heaven, but I want you to talk to God and make sure they are happy up there. I cried all month after the accident, but Roy and Margaret took me in and take care of me now and they love me and I love them. Can you ask God to protect them? I don't want to lose them too.

Benjamin

P.S. Also pray for my baby cousin Sara, in the picture.

A teardrop forms at the corner of each of my eyes. The joy in the boy's heart despite what happened to him is overwhelming. I lost my parents at an age older than his, and look at me now. I'm a wreck.

Benjamin still has trust and love towards God regardless of what happened. How can such a kid be so faithfully committed to something he can neither see, smell, nor touch? I'm eighteen and *I* don't even have that.

My tears flow down to my lips. My sobs take control over my chest. I manage to stuff them down to whimpers, but they're still audible. This is the first time I've cried in nine years. I wonder how many tears have been stored by now, like water held back by a dam.

I crumple the edges of the paper in my knuckled fists, hoping the horrible memories don't flow back in my mind. Hearing my sobs, Gammy walks in the room.

"What's wrong?" she asks delicately.

I look down at the letter in my fist, hesitating. I wipe away my tears and pull back the edges of the paper, flattening out the wrinkles. I smoothen it and hold it up weakly at her. "I want to pray for this one," I tell her without even realizing I spoke. The words escaped my mouth, climaxed by my own emotions. For a moment I try to take my words back, but then I realize I don't want to. I really *do* want to pray for Benjamin.

A meek smile forms on Gammy's lips. Her eyes sparkle and become glossy in their teary wetness. There's an expression on her face that I can't exactly pinpoint, but the word to describe it dances at the tip of my tongue, teasing me to reach for it.

"Oh, Jeremy," she says. She comes towards me and embraces me in her arms. I don't understand why she's getting so emotional, even though I have my own reasons to be. I sob weakly as she hugs me tightly. I hug back with the same hold as hers.

She steps away and gives me a big smile, twitching at her lips. The same expression remains on her face, softening her cheeks and broadening her eyes. I recognize it now.

It's hope.

Chapter 12

So we prayed. And of course it wasn't nearly as bad as I expected. To be honest, it actually felt pretty good. The feeling it gave me, knowing that I was thinking of others (or another) instead of just myself for once, and taking a personal responsibility for their well being was overwhelming. Once we began to pray, the tears ceased to flow. I didn't know praying could be so simple. It was easier than talking to a friend who wants to listen.

We hold hands tightly, facing each other, and Gammy begins to recite what she calls "The Lord's Prayer." She stops after each sentence, long enough for me to repeat her words. I clear my thoughts of everything other than the boy, Benjamin.

Those words feel wholesome and just right as they flow out of my lips.

In my prayers dedicated to him, I know that I'm also praying for myself, comparing the events of his parents' death to my own. Emotionally, I ask for a lending hand to guide Benjamin away from the path that I've decided to take. *Take care of him, God,* I say in my thoughts, as if I knew who or what I was talking to. *Make sure his love for life and for you doesn't end like mine did.* Somehow, like an odd truth that's always been known, I can feel Him listening to me. I understand his care suddenly, and I accept it.

For the past two months I kept asking myself if God existed. Somehow now I'm able to answer that for myself. Maybe this is a big step—recognizing his existence—but this also brings out so many more topics and questions that I still can't grasp, neither physically nor mentally. It brings up the type of questions journalists try to answer and explain to their audience through an article. All these questions begin with "Who?", "What?", "Why?", "When?", "Where?", and especially, "How?"

How is it all possible? How does he look out for us? How are we so oblivious to Him most of the time?

When we're finally finished praying, Gammy squeezes my hands tighter and then lets go. In that moment I can feel the delicate softness of her palms. I look up at her face and that reassuring presence of hope still lingers around her face with a pleasant fit.

I feel strange inside now. What is that? What is this feeling? It seems to make my chest tumble in its own self and make my veins yodel.

I think it's relief.

I know I can read more letters now, and I want to. Suddenly I feel as if I need to read more because I want to expand that sense of relief. I felt like I was lying under a mountain of rocks before, and one by one they're being picked off my chest for each letter I read.

This is an addiction I think I could love.

Quickly, and as neatly as I can manage, I put all the already-opened letters aside into several stacks of paper. Pushing envelopes, pictures and papers out of the way, I reach for the second plastic bag holding about five more pounds of mail.

I burrow one hand through the letters, deciding to pick the next one at random. I yank out the predestined letter, and a few others come of out the bag along with it. With curiosity, I turn the little rectangular piece of paper around in my grasp and read the return mail address. It's from Benjamin, this time the address written in orange crayon.

Impatiently I tear the envelope open and pinch the edge of the letter. I pull it out carefully, and another three-hole-punched, lined notebook sheet of paper appears. Benjamin's letter is shorter this time. There's a single sentence sprawled horizontally across the page.

Thank you for praying for me Jeremy, my mom just told me in my dream.

My body becomes neutralized, numbed like an elephant shot by a tranquilizer. The letter falls from grasp, zigzagging in midair until it reaches the ground.

Chapter 13

All this mail must be getting to me. I had to have imagined reading what I did. Slowly I bend over to pick up the piece of paper off the floor, and my head swarms as if diving through a pool of mercury. A sharp dot of pain burrows through my forehead and reached all the way through to the back of my head.

I read the short message again, and it's the same as before.

Benjamin had known I would pray for him before I actually did. Is that possible? Or could he have just dreamt his mom telling him that I did, turning out to be just a coincidence. Quite a coincidence, though.

I put aside all the shoeboxes and letters, deciding not to read any more. All of this is too much to take in all at once. I push aside the remaining shopping bags left to read, deciding that I need a break. The rest, I can read later.

My mug of hot chocolate with baby marshmallows has become lukewarm, and certainly lost its purpose. I pour the thick liquid down the drain, and rinse the large mug in the sink.

The phone rings, drilling into the stiffened silence. I hesitate for a moment, afraid of who it could be on the other end. Some stubborn journalist, maybe. Could even be an NBC agent inviting me as a guest on Conan O'Brien or Jay Leno. Could be *20/20*. ABC. CBS. CNN. God knows who else has me on their hit list. Something in me though, tells me it's not any of them.

I hesitate, looking at the phone and hearing it scream for my attention one more time. I step closer to it, and finally I curl the receiver in my grasp, bringing it up to my ear. "Hu-hello?" I ask with a quivering tone.

"Hey, is—Jeremy?" the voice asks, alarmed.

"Who is this?" My voice sounds strangely testy.

"It's me, Ben."

"Benjamin?" I ask, yelling into the phone.

"Only my mom calls me that. What wrong with you? Why are you screaming? Hello? You there?"

"Yeah, yeah, I'm here," I say relieved and feeling a little embarrassed. "Sorry, I'm a bit jumpy tonight." Even though I really have no reason to be, I realize.

"No shit. Didn't notice. Listen, I'm having a few people over tonight. Some already showed up. You wanna come?"

"No, that's all right. I don't feel like going out tonight. Not in the mood."

"Are you sure? Buncha girls are here."

"Which girls?" I ask, still not very interested in the offer.

"Well, for one, Jessica Davis is on the couch looking cute as a button." He makes a baby voice at this, and then resumes his normal voice again. "You want me to put her on?"

"What time?" I say.

"Now, if you want."

I slam down the phone and head for the door. I don't think any other girl could have gotten me to the door so fast, but Jessica, holy-moly sweet boloney, if angels were visiting Earth, she'd be one of them.

"I'm heading out, Gammy!" I shout to her as I slip one arm through my coat sleeve. I grab a winter tussle cap, and put it over my head, covering the tips of my ears. Romulus approaches me, wagging his tail from side to side like a whip. "No, boy," I tell him, "I'm not taking you for a walk." I pull my gloves over my hands and begin to turn the doorknob.

"Right now?" she asks.

Romulus lifts his nose, pointing it towards the door and barks.

"Yeah, can I?" I say with one foot already outside the door. Showing through the foggy window, thousands of puffy flakes precipitate to the ground, adding up to the inches of snow that have already settled.

"I'm just going to Ben's." I add, "It's a five-minute walk."

"All right, that's fine. You're all wrapped up, so I don't have to worry about you getting cold, I guess. Have fun."

Romulus barks again, this time more aggressively. His tail stops wagging and he curls his lips to show teeth. He barks once more, even louder than before. This time he adds an unmistakably threatening growl to it.

"What's wrong with you?" I ask him, not expecting a response. Romulus looks at me, softening his look, and whines. Then he shifts his gaze back at the door, which I'm still holding by the handle waiting for Gammy's approval to head out, and growls nastily at its direction. His eyes are fixed. I pat him on his head, but now he doesn't even acknowledge me.

"Don't be home too late," she tells me, sighing uneasily.

"No later than four in the morning, Gammy, don't you worry," I tell her while slipping out the door. I catch a glimpse of her smiling before shutting the door behind me. Romulus sprints for his chance at escape, hoping to chase away whatever animal must have gotten his attention, but I push him back with a hand and manage to keep him inside. He starts barking loudly and scratching at the door, hopelessly trying to get out or to get my attention. He moves to the window and continues to bark at my general direction. This time the yaps come through repetitively, following one after the other.

I zip up my coat, covering up from the freezing cold air, and try to ignore him. I snag my hat down another inch or so, and I pull the hood over my head for the extra layer of warmth. My steps slush through the snow-layered walkway, knowing that I'll have to shovel it again in the morning.

The night has darkened to a deeper, more obscure black, illuminated only by the falling flakes of snow that reflect whatever light they can grasp. They fall down in swarming swoops, racing one another to see which one can reach the ground first. On the street, a large truck passes by like a rumbling snail, spreading salt into hundreds of different flinging directions. In front of it, a metal pale pushes the crumbly snow to the side. It turns a corner and then disappears both in sound and in sight.

As I step past the mailbox, a chill grazes my neck like the cold hand of a demon. My skin tenses, bringing me to a hard shiver, the kind you'd think that I was shaking water off of me. A sinking, odd feeling draws to my throat as I swallow a thin gleam of saliva. The feeling drops suddenly to my chest, and then warmly scrapes at my stomach, forming an odd, uncomfortable contrast in temperatures.

I've had this sort of feeling before, when walking into Mass late and knowing that everyone's eyes were watching us. A cold shiver runs up my spine in a snakelike glide, biting down with each crawling inch. I look around, and of course I see no one. The feeling remains though, bold and strong. It's impossible to ignore. I walk a little faster, boosted by an energy filled with paranoia. The streets are slushy, and the salted snow begins to seep through my shoes, making my feet feel colder by the second. I should've worn boots.

A rustling sound comes from behind me. I don't turn. I don't dare to. Instead my steps scurry even faster, my pant legs zip-zapping against one another.

Before long, I find myself jogging. It's cold outside, I try to convince myself, and I'm just trying to get to Ben's house quicker. But I can't fool myself. I know exactly why I'm moving so fast, and I'm sure that whoever is following me knows it too.

To my right side, a long stream of neatly trimmed bushes stretches along the edge of the road. I jog parallel to it, keeping my distance. With each step I take, more and more rustling noises make themselves heard, coming from the hedges. My heart thumps at a cadence double that of my running steps.

I stop jogging. This is ridiculous. Just moments after I stop, the rustling noises do too.

"Hello?" I ask no one, and no answer follows in its reply. "Hello?" I scream louder. "Is someone there?"

But there's nobody there, Jeremy! It's all in your head. You're just getting paranoid. But this thought doesn't comfort me in the slightest bit of conviction. I don't confide myself in those words.

A cold breeze slaps into my face, fluttering my hood and making my face pinch tightly. I squint my eyes shut and reopen them once the blow has passed. I stand in the middle of the street, looking at the hedges, watching carefully to see if they should move.

You're not imagining things, I tell myself, but it feels like a different voice is speaking to me. You're not insane. Those bushes were moving. You *did* hear them.

Everything is still except for the snow dropping in flakes of disaster. Even the breeze has paused, waiting for me to make my move. *Draw*, I feel like the revolving silence is telling me, like those old Western movies where two men stand before a gun battle. The setting is all wrong though, and the other gunslinger seems to be hiding.

Taking a step towards the hedges, I'm shaking so furiously that everything I tell myself is a lie. I want to know where the noises came from. I want to know what's behind there.

But you don't! Just leave! That other voice screams at me.

There has to be something behind there, even if just an animal. That noise had been following me, so it couldn't have been the wind rustling the leaves.

An animal? In this cold?

Something, then. I need to know what it is.

No. You don't.

I take one more step closer, and the other voice gives up. My mind's a blank beyond reasoning. This time the snow cheats me, crunching beneath my foot instead of its original sloshing sound. The streets are isolated and invisible here, the light doesn't reach, which is nearly everywhere. Only the presence of that deadly sound—which for now lays dormant in secrecy—and I occupy the dark night.

I stand still for another moment, trying to gather up enough courage to take the next step. I hear a wheezing laughter, one inside my head—I think—mocking my curiosity. My foot lifts, ready to approach my third step. Suddenly that noise resumes itself to life, sounding twice as agitated as before. The leaves shake and the twigs crackle with furious malice. Whoever is hiding behind the bushes knows that I've discovered him, or her, and wants me to run. It's trying to scare me.

Fighting my own fears, I walk closer and closer to the possessed bushes.

With each closing step, the rustling gets louder and louder. My heart pounds at my chest, imploring me to turn away, but my curiosity muffles its sound. I'm just one step away from being able to peer over the bushes, and now my breaths are no more than fast pants, ravished by the intense pumps of my withering lungs. My foot rises, prepared to fulfill its motion, but just before it can reach the crunching snow again, a screeching hiss bursts out, declaring its threat. This time, I know the sound isn't inside my own head. The hiss is keen with torment, scratching at the air like nails on a chalkboard. It's a sound so horrifying that it could create images to haunt one's nightmares for nights to come.

I don't want to know what's behind those hedges anymore. I turn to run, but my feet's grip on the slick ground falters, bringing me down to my hands and knees. I push up with my arms and take off running, hoping that I won't slip again. From behind, I hear something jump out from the hedges and following after me. I run faster, too afraid to look back, and for each step I take, I pray that it won't fail me. The thumping of running feet follows so closely that they might as well be the echo of my own steps.

With all my energy, I kick harder with my legs, and my thighs assume a locomotive flow of motion. Soon, the motion overlaps itself, running at full speed, not having to force my body in motion anymore. My entire body is locked in this uncontrollable stride, guzzling an adrenaline-powered rush. I don't think I could even stop myself if I tried. In my own dazed fear I try to hear if the creature—by now I'm convinced that whatever made that hissing sound couldn't have been human—is still chasing behind.

It is.

I take a cornered right at the first intersection, bringing me on Ben's street. I find myself still running at my fastest and unable to stop, both because of fear and due to my momentum.

I reach Ben's driveway, stepping on a wide sheet of slick ice. My legs buckle. I try to stop, but my speed has taken control over my motion, erasing any chance of stopping. Just as I'm about to slip backwards, the ice on the ground ends, and the rough concrete of the driveway starts again. The soles of my shoes grip on the rough ground. My balance resumes, but then I'm thrust forward out of control. My face smacks against the garage door, denting it inward. The hollow banging sound that follows resonates the air in an exploding boom. The sound blurs into my head, and then pierces through like a needle popping air pockets in my brain.

I let gravity take its toll, and I lay on the ground long enough for my blurry vision to come back to focus. I shake my head, and quickly the shapes of things become recognizable again. I sit up, with my palms to the frozen ground, and I find myself covered in light. The sensor lights had turned on when I slid in the driveway.

Beyond the driveway, just out of reach of the light, I see a darkened outline of a figure watching me. Its shoulders are slumped forward with the hands nearly reaching down to the kneecaps. Its face is shaded over, but the eyes are still visible. They seem to glow, even though they're only reflecting the light that falls just beyond them. These eyes—these round, cocooned and placid eyes—they smolder two pale yellow torches into the dark. The creature grins horribly at me.

It stands alone, unmoving, accompanied by its best friend, the night. The creature seems more than pleased by the darkness and doesn't dare take a step closer to the driveway cascaded by light.

"Who the hell's out there?" a voice shouts from my right. Disturbed by Ben's voice, the creature runs off on all fours. In a matter of seconds, it disappears into its abyss, going back to wherever it came from.

"It's me," I shout up at him from the ground. "I slid on some ice and crashed against your garage door."

"You all right?"

"Yeah, I'm fine. I'm just a little banged up."

"Well come on in! Join the fun."

I stand up, and I walk up the short steps that lead to the front door. Just before stepping inside his house, I look back one last time and see nothing more than the snow-plagued night.

Chapter 14

I step inside the living room and the place is filled with people. Almost everyone is either holding a beer in their hand or a lit pipe, with the cherry burning bright red with each puff. A group of girls stand by the stereo, looking at CDs and yapping to one another. Their faces are all too recognizable. Ben and I call them "the Dixie chicks with hardcore dicks" because they're always looking for guys to fulfill the second part of that statement. I don't even have to listen in to know that they're sharing stories of the where and the who with.

One of them, Elisa I think her name is, is wearing a pair of tight black leather pants and a shirt with grooves cut into it that barely covers her nipples. No bra. I don't want to venture a guess about her panties. Likely, she's wearing a thong that says "fuck me hardcore" that either speaks for itself or actually says it in written letters.

So Elisa yaps her mouth open and shut, flaunting about which guy it was this time, where they did it, and how they pulled it off without having to call herself a slut, I presume. Then I hear one of the other girls shout back at her, "You bitch! That's *my* guy!"

These girls, they're an itching sensation. You'll itch at night, drinks blurring your senses, wanting to get your hands on one of them and something else inside them. They're cute girls, after all. Round eyes, hot lips, narrow faces. Typical, but cute. There's a selection to choose from amongst them, and a few are better off than the others, but if you're not the picky kind then any one of them will do. Especially if you're drunk. The itch, though, will follow over to the morning sometimes—when you'll be scratching your balls for the next few days until you finally figure out that something's not right.

Most of the time, they're not so picky themselves. Usually, they're more than earnest and willing to take off their already-too-revealing shirts off just so that you can offer them a drink and tell them how gorgeous they are. I guess giving a girl attention can get you pretty far into...well you know—*them.*

One of the girls seems awfully familiar. Then I see that it's Tara, my little one night stand from that Friday night in April. She looks up at me, offers a double take, and then looks away with a flash of recognition in her eyes. She looks back at the girls and continues her conversation.

I look around to the other side of the room, and I see Jessica smiling away to a few people I never met before. She's sitting on the couch, with her legs pressed closed and her hands on her thighs. Every once in a while she'll raise and flutter a hand to make a point, and then back down on her lap.

"You want a beer?" Ben asks, yanking at my shirt before I can advance Jessica.

"No, I'm good." I say, noticing that Jessica isn't drinking, deciding that I shouldn't either. "I know where to get one if I change my mind." When Ben's parents are gone at his house, there's always either a keg on ice in some corner of the living room or stacks of beer in the fridge. Sometimes both. Not to mention that the cabinets are always filled with the finest selection of cheap liquor. That stuff is what the Dixie chicks usually help themselves to when trying to impair their own judgment.

I approach Jessica slowly. She's wearing a long pair of jeans and a small hooded sweatshirt with a picture of a pink bunny on the front. The bunny says "You make me puke a little." Her glance turns to me. She smiles with her curved lips stretching and says, "Are you a little cold there, Jeremy?"

"Huh?" I say, but then realize I'm still wearing my coat, gloves and tussle cap. "Oh" is all I can get out. I give her a quick smile, and begin to pull off my cap and gloves and stuff them inside one of my larger coat pockets. She shifts aside, giving me room to sit next to her. I oblige, unzipping my coat and peeling the cap off my head.

"What'd you do to yourself, sweetie?" She gets close to me, trying to inspect my forehead. I bring my hand to where she's looking at, feeling a bump. I look at my fingers and the tips have droplets of blood on them.

"That's not good. Does it look bad?" I say.

"Could be worse. What happened?"

Thinking back to what just happened outside, my words come out slowly and insecure. "I…slipped…and banged my head."

She laughs and gives me a suspicious look. "That doesn't sound very convincing. What *really* happened?"

"No, it's the truth. Did you hear that loud bang from outside?"

"That was *you*?"

"Yeah, I slid on a sheet of ice on Ben's driveway, and I smacked face first against his garage door."

"That sounded like a *really* big bang!"

"Yeah, I was running."

"What were you running for?" she asks with a hint of curiosity peeking up from the tip of her voice.

I hesitate, trying to think of the right words that won't make me sound either stupid or ridiculous. "Well, I'm not a hundred percent sure, but I think I was being followed."

"Followed?" she says, her voice tinted by intrigue, "By who?"

"I don't even know. I was just walking over here from my house, and somebody was hiding behind the bushes." I can just hear myself now. What am I saying? "I could hear the leaves rustling, so I went to take a look. Then someone…" "Someone" isn't exactly the right word to describe the thing that I saw though. The right word is more like "creature," but I couldn't say that without sounding like some sort of deranged lunatic. "…jumped out and began chasing after me. I just ran."

"That's creepy. Was it a reporter?"

"Could be…" But I didn't believe it.

"You should put a Band-Aid on it or something," she says, still looking at the cut on my head.

"Yeah, I think I'll do that. I'll be right back." I get up from the seat, hating to have to leave her behind even if for just a second.

"Don't be gone long," she tells me with a sweet and irresistible smile and a hand reaching for my fingertips.

I walk around, making my way through the crowd and excusing myself. Then from behind me, a soft hand grabs my arm. I assume it's Jessica, so I turn around smiling. My smile drops when I see the very last person I'd ever want to talk to.

"Hi," the pale-skinned, dirty blonde-haired girl tells me with an irritating smirk stamped on her lips. Her chin is butt-ended but pinched, like a permanently settled dimple. In her hand she's half limpidly holding a drink to her chest, tilting it forwards without realizing that if it were to tip any more it would spill.

"Hello, Megan," I tell her flatly, tainted by a bit of cynicism. Just the *thought* of my ex-girlfriend being here makes my balls feel like they're being clenched inside someone's fist, but actually *seeing* her in front of me with that ridiculous smirk on her face is more like having a vice tightening down on them instead. "What are you doing here?" I ask her as I approach the bathroom door. "I'm sure you weren't invited."

"Nobody gets invited to parties. They just show up." Her words are slurred together, obvious that the drink in her hand isn't her first. She approaches closer and her breaths draft out like winded spirits, pungent with the smells of candy apple schnapps mixed in with a hint of peppermint vodka. "We haven't seen each other in over a month. So now that you're all famous, you're too busy to call me?" she says pouting, placing her abrasive hand on my arm. I take a step back from her.

"I told you I wouldn't call. We broke up, remember?"

"No," she tells me with her index finger raised up as if she's about to make an impressive point, "I broke up with *you.*" At "you" she points her finger at me, laughing an odd little giggle as if she were in on a joke that I must be oblivious to. She guzzles down a gulp of what looks like orange juice, and then squints her face tightly as she swallows.

"What do you want?" I ask her. By now I've stepped inside the bathroom, and I'm looking out at her through the door's threshold.

"Well," she tells me, trying to sound charming and sexy, only failing and sounding more like a drunken hooker, "I missed you this past month. I never got to see you except for on the news. And I was thinking that maybe we should get back together. What do you think about that? I've been horny for you all week, and now that we're here maybe we can work that off me." She bites down on her lower lip and reaches out with her hand to rub my chest.

"Sorry, but I've got to use the bathroom for a second," I tell her, as I swing the door shut. She stops the door's motion with her foot and steps forward.

"I don't mind to watch," she tells me, as her hand creeps down below my belt line, into my pants. Her grip tightens, but remains gentle enough not to hurt. I grab her hand back out in disgust.

"I'm just looking for a Band-Aid. I don't need your help." Suddenly it feels like the Band-Aid was a horrible idea after all.

"We can look for it together," she says in a husky voice, trying to sound seductive. She takes another gulp and grimaces at the taste of her screwdriver.

"Maybe you don't know what 'looking for a Band-Aid' means because I think we have two different ideas in mind. It's a one-man job, and I'm sure I can handle it without your frisky hands getting in the way. Oh, and I think it would be a *horrible* idea if we got back together." I try to make those last words come out as crisp, as clear, and as piercing as possible. Finally the message gets across the deranged brain of the girl standing before me, and her face turns to a drunken angry expression.

"Fine!" she screams at my face while flinging her hands like crows scattering in the air, spilling most of what's left of her drink. Her breath fumigates the small bathroom, filling it with the stench of a bar's blends of liquors, strong enough to cause secondhand drunkenness. She rushes out of the bathroom, and people passing by look at me weirdly. I turn around and open the medicine cabinet in search of what I came in here to look for. I find two boxes, and only the one holding jumbo Band-Aids has anything left in it. I throw away the empty box in the little trashcan and stick one of the huge squares of cloth on my forehead.

Back in the living room I find Jessica, and I sit back down on the couch where she has my seat saved for me. "How do I look?" I ask her.

"Ridiculous," she says laughing. "It looks like you put an eye patch to cover your third eye."

"That's all right then, 'cuz I thought it looked more like a pad for a moment." We both laugh.

Softly she puts her hand over my own and stands up, pulling me along gently. I get up with her and ask, "Where are we going?"

"Outside," she tells me, "where we can be alone. It's too loud in here."

"Aren't you going to be cold?"

"You can keep me warm." She smiles. I follow behind her, and we head outside on the porch where the lounge chairs and a table are covered by hills of white snow. I grab one of the chairs and shake all the snow off. Jessica switches on a light, and for a minute we admire the tiny crystals dancing in the air as if the night sky were their ballroom of winded music.

I lay down on the chair, and she sits beside me. We squeeze close together, holding one another as if afraid of falling off this world.

For hours we talk about the most meaningless and the most meaningful things that come to mind. We throw ideas at one another, and the words flow out beautifully, like releasing butterflies from their glass jars. I don't even have to make an effort in keeping up with my share of the conversation. We talk about our fears, our passions, our dreams, our futures, and of everything else in between, leaving nothing behind us left unsaid. And yet, even once all has been said, more words still manage to come out, never easing towards dull topics or raising disinterest from either of us. Every phrase that comes out feels greater and more meaningful than sex has ever had. Sex, I think, is a joke compared to this. Sex, the way I've experienced it at least. The random kind, where beggars can't be choosers and getters can't be whiners.

That's the kind of sex that holds a lie. Mainly the lie is hidden in the wails, and in moans, and sometimes in the screams of the act. It lies in the moment of climax, in the moment of orgasm, and in the withdrawal. The lie that two people share in this astray of sex is "I need you," when what they both really mean is "I want you."

In sex, during the peak to its ultimate gratification, the one you're with doesn't even seem to matter. She disappears without you even having to close your eyes. It's a "me" factor that takes over just then, screaming to scratch that itch of self-gratification. Another push. Another pump. Another thrust, and you think that it'll all be fantastic. It will be all right. It'll be tolerable. It might not be so bad.

But even then, all you want is still more. It's like following a string into the darkness, thinking that if you yank hard enough the tug will bring you to its end.

But it doesn't.

That tug weaves you through a dazed wonder and slaps you in the face with withering want. And just when you think that she's disappeared, your partner in crime, your sex goddess in gospel of lust, your muffled yet screaming mistress—there she comes back again. And in that moment you want to possess her, except you lie to both yourself and to her and you say "need" her instead. You *need* to possess her. You *need* for her to be yours.

84

Writhing…screaming…moaning…squirming—all things you think you've created through the power of your own sex drive—and you *need* them back. You need for her to scream your name. You need for her to need you.

Then it happens. And it stops.

The need subsides, and instead you're left with a slither of self-disgust. But only for a moment. A short moment—not long enough for you to have learned your lesson. Not long enough to teach you that your needs weren't at all satisfied, because if they had been you wouldn't have to come back for more.

But then you're stuck, holding onto the girl, the tool, the thing you thought you needed but only wanted, becoming no different than a child wanting a toy he'll soon throw away. So she tries to hold you close and you can't go anywhere. All you want to do is wash your face, brush your teeth, cleanse your body. But you do none of it. Instead, you lie embraced by your own vanished desires, and covered in the same sweat that moments ago you wished would never go away.

Compared to all that, Jessica's hold is bliss.

Here and now, in this bliss, in this fantastic little bliss, the world itself disappears, leaving only Jessica and me behind. Here the distinction between want and need becomes clear; it isn't blurred by my own suffocating desires. In holding Jessica, it's impossible to forget that she's right here, sharing my heat and grazing my cheek with her own. The "me" factor doesn't play a role in any of this. In talking to her and hugging her tightly, *she's* the one I want to fulfill and satisfy.

This bliss feels more than just good. It feels right. Like a truth finally unveiled.

"Jeremy?" Jessica says, after we've finally reached the comfort of silence.

"Yeah?"

"I like this."

And I smile.

Chapter 15

"Truth or dare," Ben says with strings of cheese stretching out from his mouth. He blows with his lips to cool the bite of pizza he just took.

Ben and I are sitting at a booth at Luciano's pizza lounge. The restaurant is dimly lit, and a hazy fog of cigarette smoke lingers in the air from the earlier customers. Ben takes a sip of his pink lemonade, and then fans his mouth with his hand. "Damn that's hot," he says.

"'Truth or dare'?" I repeat unsurely, wondering if I heard him right. "What are we, in fifth grade?"

"Come on, man, truth or dare. When was the last time you played that?"

"Probably before I had hair on my balls."

"So since yesterday?"

"You're a funny one. Anyone ever tell you that?" We both laugh. A small chunk of cheese and red sauce falls from his lips.

"Humor me and answer the question," he says.

"You're supposed to play with girls, so you have them do things they normally wouldn't."

"Just play along. Truth or dare?"

I think it over for a second, then say, "Truth."

"Man, you're no fun," he says, pretending to be disappointed. "Okay, let me think of a question...You have a thing for Jessica, don't you?"

"It's that obvious?" I say smiling, blushing a little.

"Well yeah, but is it that you wanna get with her or just get in her pants?"

"No, I'm done with that," I say, lounging back in our booth.

"Done with what?" he says, tilting his face at an angle, uncertain.

"Sex. At least I think I'm done."

"What?" He bursts out laughing, holding a fist to his mouth as if he were afraid of food coming out of it. "You're not done fucking. It's what you do best."

"No, I'm serious," I say, but still smiling along with his laugh.

"Why? What made you decide that."

"Jessica."

He imitates the sound and gesture of a whip lashing. "Wha-pshh!"

"No, it's not like that. It's not like she's telling me not to have sex anymore. We never even talked about that, really. It's just that when I'm with her, I feel different. I'm not all horny and shit. It feels so good to be around her that I don't need to be messing around, you know?"

"I guess. If you say so, man," he says dubiously.

"All right, now your turn. Truth or dare?"

"Dare," he says without hesitating.

"Okay. When I tell you to—"

"You have to say, 'I dare you to...'" he says, cutting me off.

"What? No, man, that doesn't matter."

"Yeah it does. It's the rules. You have to say, 'I dare you to,' or else it's not official."

"All right, all right, whatever. Without looking, I dare you to reach out your hand and smack the next ass that comes by."

"Oh, so you give up fucking, but you're gonna have *me* smack a waitress' ass?"

"I never said it was going to be a waitress. Okay, here she comes behind you. Don't look. I'll tell you when..." I wait a moment and then say, "Now."

Ben swings his arm out, and his hand swats an ass in dark blue jeans. A heavyset man wearing a Harley Davidson jacket and a long, grizzly beard turns to him. The man looks down at Ben with icy eyes and tight lips.

"Sorry," Ben says quickly. "There was a fly, but I got it."

"Right on my ass, you did," the man says grumbling, and then walks away muttering to himself.

I burst out laughing. My laughter wails in fluttered flaps of ridiculous delight. I go on until tears come squeezed out from my eyes. Ben joins in with me, saying, "I can't believe you made me do that." He mouths the words between chuckles, struggling to get them all out. I bury my face in my arms, laughing uncontrollably.

Minutes later, when we finally stop, Ben says, "Okay, okay. Truth or dare?"

"Dare," I say, wiping tears from my eyes.

"You see that stop sign over there?" He points out the window behind me. "I dare you to run from here, to there, and then to my car..."

"*That's* your dare?" I ask, unimpressed.

"...naked," he finally finishes.

"Oh. You know how *cold* it is outside? I'm gonna get cholera!"

"Bronchitis. Cholera's when you drink sewage water," he corrects me, still smiling.

"That's what I meant. Either way, I'm not streaking out there. It's freezing!"

"That's what makes the dare funny. I had to smack that biker guy's ass! So you *have to* do this."

"Ah, man, I don't know. Running out there doesn't sound like the best idea in the world." I look outside where the wind howls and thousands of flakes shoot across in diagonals. "Do it with me," I say. "I dare you to do it with me. And we can wear our boots, 'cuz I don't feel like getting my feet frozen to the ground."

"Sounds fair."

"How are we going to pull this off?"

"We'll go in the bathroom and strip in the stalls. Then we run out, throw our clothes in my car, run to the stop sign, and then back."

"All right. Let's pay for the slices first. I don't want them to think we're ditching the check."

So we take our last quick bites and throw a few bills on the table. In the bathroom we each take a stall and start taking off our clothes, dropping them to the ground.

"No peeking!" Ben says, laughing his silly ass off.

"You ready? I'm done."

"Kay, on the count of three. One...two...three!"

Our stall doors burst open, and we bolt out holding our clothes in our arms. We run past the waitresses and one of the bus boys. The girls start whistling, while the manager shouts, "What the hell?"

"They're nudey! They're nudey, Mom!" a little girl giggles to her parents. Aw crap, I didn't think there'd be kids watching. We run faster, pushing our way out the front door. We take a right towards Ben's Mustang, open the doors, throw the clothes in and turn towards the stop sign.

Already I can feel the cold biting on my tensed skin with its silvery teeth. My lips and ears fall to warm numbness, and my teeth clatter like loose dentures being shaken.

"Oh shit it's cold. Oh shit it's cold," Ben says, running as fast as he can.

We're just steps away from the stop sign when we hear tires grinding on the ice, screeching to a stop. "Benjamin?" a woman's voice shouts from behind. "Jeremy?" she then adds, unsure. I turn just before touching the stop sign, with Ben a few paces behind.

Our boots slide on the iced pavement, and we turn.

"Mrs. Norton?" I say.

"Oh shit, Mom," Ben adds.

I stand there, shivering and cupping my junk with my hands. Ben walks closer to the stopped car, a new Audi, and leans over the window.

"What are you, crazy?" Ben's mom screams, sounding like a woman being cheated out of her bingo winnings.

"Hello, Mr. Norton." I toss Ben's father a quick wave. He does the same while sitting at the wheel.

"Jeremy." He nods, acknowledging me. "A little cold to be running around naked, don't you think?"

"Don't you humor them!" Mrs. Norton snaps at her husband.

"Mom, you've seen me naked before, what's the big deal?" Ben says, trying to calm her down.

"Yes, *I* have, but not the entire city of Detroit!"

By now people have gathered around to watch from a safe distance, giggling and whispering to one another. A girl of about our age points at us. I wave back at her with a quick gesture and a smile that says, *Do you mind?*

"Hey, Jeremy, listen, come over for dinner some time. We haven't seen much of you lately," Mr. Norton shouts over Ben's argument with his mother. And I'm sure now you've seen way too much.

"Sure will," I say politely.

"Aw, come on. They're just kids, Katrina," Mr. Norton says to his wife, trying to calm her down. "Let them have their fun."

"We'll talk about this when you get home, Ben!" his mom screams at him.

"Okay, Mom. Bye!"

"Don't you 'bye' me! Listen! Come here so I can talk to you a minute! Come here!"

"Bye, Mom! Dad, could you please drive off?"

And so the Audi drives away, ending the show for the viewers on the street.

"Man, what a bitch!" Ben says to me, as we walk back to his car, shivering.

Chapter 16

Gammy is in the living room tidying up. She fluffs the pillows on the couch, straightens the rug on the floor, and dusts around.

"Are you having people over?" I ask her.

"Yes, stay awhile. Someone is coming over to talk to us."

Then there's a knock at the door. Gammy finishes off quickly, and scoots to the door to answer it. As she opens it, a flurry of snowflakes flies in.

"I couldn't find the door bell," the man at the door says to Gammy with a smile. He opens his heavy button-up coat, and below it he's wearing a black shirt neatly tucked into a sharply ironed pair of black pants. Then I notice the white collar around his neck. He's the priest from St. Regis' Church.

"That's all right, we don't have one." Gammy says. "Come in. Let me take your coat."

"Thank you." As he steps in, he adjusts the small oval glasses on his nose. Then he pulls off the blue tussle cap and pats down the gray hair around his balded head.

"So glad you could come, Father. Coffee or hot chocolate?" Gammy waves him towards the couch after putting his coat in the closet. Then she scoots towards the kitchen before even getting an answer.

"Hot chocolate would be great," he says loud enough so that she can hear. Then he turns to me. "Jeremy!" He gives me the smile of a long lost friend and holds out a hand for me, reaching his arm over the coffee table. I take his hand and he squeezes it with a tight grip, but his hand is soft, and his skin smooth.

"Nice to meet you, Mister...?" I say, still shaking his hand.

"Father Birmingham, actually. But you can call me John, Father John, Johnny-O, or whatever you prefer," he says joyfully, with his face still stretching out a smile

"You were there that day, weren't you?"

"The day of the miracle? Yes, yes, that'd be me. As you could tell, I was rather shocked! I had a hard time finishing Mass after you walked out." He gives a quick, good-humored laugh. We sit on the couch, both of us taking an end.

He lounges comfortably with his hands on his knees, keeping his attention towards me.

"Why *did* you finish Mass? I mean, I wouldn't have. I don't think I could have."

"It's a rule of the Church. Once Mass begins, it has to be carried through to the end. Much like the saying, 'The show must go on.'"

"Oh I see," I say, nodding.

"Gosh you look so much like your father."

"You knew my dad?"

"We met during one of the rougher parts of my life and became good friends after that. He was a very good man."

"I never knew that. I mean, the part of you two being friends."

"You know, Jeremy, you were the first miracle I've witnessed in my life. Of that great caliber, I mean. I find it to be a huge blessing! Only three hundred people in the *world* had a chance to see it, and I was one of them!" As he talks, his hands move and wave, emphasizing his words with casual gestures. "I didn't recognize you at first because after Trevor and Barbara died I lost touch with your family, other than with your grandma. But I was not surprised when I saw that it was you who delivered the message. You come from a very wonderful family, and your parents were the most generous and loving people I ever had a chance to meet."

Gammy walks back with a small round tray in her hands. She hands a cup of chocolate to Father Birmingham and the other to me, keeping the mug of coffee to herself. Then she sits down on the armchair, facing us.

Father Birmingham continues, "The Awakening, as the Holy Father decided to call it, is putting a lot of questions on many people's minds. Did you know, that for weeks after that day in April, people came to me, shouting and accusing me of fixing the whole thing up?"

"I read that in the newspaper. What did you tell them?"

"I told them the truth, of course. I told them what I knew, and that was all I *could* tell them."

"Did they believe you?"

"On the most part…no. People are very hard to get through at times. If they have their minds fixed on something, there's not much you can do to change that. But then also came those who believed in the miracle and the message you spoke. And they were the ones with the most questions."

"Like what?"

"Well," he says uneasily, turning his hands palms up, "this is a very tough situation, so the number of questions were infinite. Too many to recall all of them. But the one question that kept coming up was, 'How should we prepare?'" He pauses a moment, nodding silently to the question. "Unfortunately, God's message didn't reveal the answer to that, so I wasn't certain on what to tell them. But then, I thought back and reviewed what the message did say.

"By analyzing the message, I came up with three things that it *does* tell us. We know *when* Judgment will begin: on the first day of July. We know how *long* it will last: forty days and forty nights. And finally, we know what we must *do* during those days: remain inside our houses. So then the question became easier to answer. To prepare spiritually, of course, we must pray and keep praying. But to prepare physically, we must have enough food and supplies that will last us for the duration of Judgment. It is said in the Bible, of course, that man does not live on bread alone, but only men and women with immense faiths would be able to last those forty days without even a single crumb of bread. Jesus is the only man who's ever actually done it.

"Now, the physical part will be easy. All one has to do is go out to the store and buy what he needs, and honestly, I believe that if our will is strong enough, God will provide for us even if we run out of food inside our own houses. But the spiritual part won't be so easy. I wanted to talk to you personally about this to ask you to spread the word around. People need to know. I wrote an article explaining all this in depth and sent it to all the Catholic and Christian magazines I could think of, but there are many people out there who don't read that sort of material. So I need you to tell everyone you know about this, and explain exactly what they need to do. Tell your friends and anyone else who comes to you asking for advice."

"I will." Although, I don't know how easily I can fulfill that promise. I've never talked to anyone I knew about God except for Jessica. It'll be hard to bring up the subject unless they bring it up first.

"Good, good. I'm glad to see that God has chosen the right man for the job. I'm relieved to have had this talk with you."

"Thank you, Father." But the smile on my face is meek.

PANIC

Chapter 17

Yet another month has slipped through the grip of time, bringing us that much closer to our fates. Panic has struck the world with its delightful mockery of what we cannot escape, other than through death itself. Believers around the world have by now circled that fateful day on their calendars with a permanent red marker.

A rush of dread and panic gnaws at my bones each day that I awake. That feeling grows only stronger when I step outside where the jagged cold cuts through my skin. Terror clenches onto the faces of strangers who day by day cross my path on the streets. I doubt anyone wants to be out on such days where the temperatures drop with each tick of the clock, but none of us have a choice.

Constantly, the supermarkets and stores are packed with customers where day after day shoppers stock up on resources that will need to last for the forty days to come. It feels like Y2K all over again; only the sensation of terror out on the streets is more real, more dreadful and way more grabbing than how it was then. Untamed fears mock us daily, and we can't do a thing to control them. Too many believed that the Y2K scare was nothing more than big talk. Those people were able to stay cool despite all the paranoid men and women stocking up on useless supplies and buying computers that wouldn't crash like the ones they already had. Then, once the new millennium finally approached, everyone who had filled their basements with useless material was anonymously mocked by the rest. Not directly, but it was an assumed jeering.

This time things aren't the same. This time the cards have been dealt differently, and the only way to do things right this time is by doing the things that we did wrong then.

Today the roads are jammed with cars. Inside, their heaters are cranked to the max, and shivering drivers yell at other cars to get a move on. This is where Gammy and I find ourselves right now. Covered by multiple layers of clothing, we wait patiently in traffic while others press on their horns just to release their rage. In front of us, a large SUV moves up a few feet. I release the pressure from the brake and do the same. From bumper to bumper, streams of cars stretch down the road as if they were all connected to one another.

On my lap, a scatter of letters lay sprawled in their own contained cries, some opened, some not. While keeping one hand on the wheel, I read through the most recent mail that's come in the past few days. Gammy does the same in her passenger seat, helping me through all the letters that have been swarming in like the snow outside. Just until the end of May I was receiving around three to four bags of mail a day—five on Mondays—but since the beginning of June the numbers have doubled, and the screams for help have risen to shrieks, which sometimes I think I can hear lifting off the pages. Most of the letters sound deranged and couldn't even be described in words the way they make me feel. Loss of courage pushes through repeatedly in most of the letters.

Every night I've spent an hour or so praying for the men, women and children who reach out to me in search of guidance. Some of their worries rub off onto me as they describe horrible nightmares in explicit details of ghouls and demons taking away their souls to a deep and dark hole burrowing within the Earth. Some of the nightmares are so vivid and horrifying that I can't even dwell on them for more than a few seconds. I try to pray for each person individually, but eventually the work becomes too overwhelming, forcing me to wrap things up with a last thought of hope for them all.

Every once in a while I receive a letter from someone telling me how much better he or she feels since the first time they wrote me. Those come in scarce numbers, but they're the ones I take the most pride in.

Gammy taps on my shoulder and points out through the windshield. To our right the parking lot to the supermarket begins. I turn into the lot and park the car at the first spot I find, not wasting time in finding one closer to the entrance.

The traffic in the lot is just as bad as the one on the road. More honking takes place as impatient men and women become frustrated with those driving in front of them. The wind whistles at a high pitch, loud enough to engulf the sound of people screaming and cussing at one another. A coil of frozen air tugs at my coat and pants, making them flutter like loose kites.

Once inside, we see that only three shopping carts are left. We grab two and we push our way through the snow-dampened and clustered aisles. Traffic has spread its course to even inside the store, where it's impossible to get through without having to maneuver through and around the rest of the shoppers. Inside here it's as if every holiday and birthday have been packed on the same day. All of the 25 cash registers have their lamps on. The lines stretch out in snakelike waves, digging into the aisles for length.

"We'll be here all day," I tell Gammy, overstating the obvious.

"If we're lucky," she says with one hand rubbing her forehead stressfully as the other clutches onto her shopping cart, afraid that somebody might snatch it away if she didn't.

We split our grocery list in half. I scan through my half and begin to look for the aisles containing my items. As they recognize me, most of the customers make way out of respect, while some look at us with piercing eyes, nonverbally blaming me for the chaos that I've created all around.

"I'll meet you at register seven in an hour," Gammy tells me, and we split up. I look at my watch and notice that it's 9:17 in the morning. We had left the house at eight thinking that it would take no longer than half an hour to get to the supermarket.

I push my cart through the store, weaving in and out of things to avoid collision with other carts. Down aisle eight, two men argue out loud over what seems to be the last bag of pretzel sticks.

"Let go, you asshole!" one screams at the other. Thin strings of saliva fling out of his mouth as he shouts.

"No fucking way, you're not taking the last bag!" the other one answers, shouting twice as loud as the first. The two men tug at the bag from each end with one hand, making sure they don't let go of their carts. I stroll past and look at the shelves to find what I need. Most of the brand name products are already gone, leaving little choice for the rest of us who came too late.

The taller of the two men yanks harder with his grip. The second man, who's overweight and burly, lets go of his cart and makes a fist with his hand, intending to swing at the other man if he doesn't let go of his prize.

The taller man doesn't flinch. Then he turns to me, and a look of recognition comes over his face.

"Hey, Christ!" he calls out to me as if I were one of his college buddies. Slowly I turn to him, swinging my cart around, almost sideswiping a little girl who comes running by. "Which one of us should have this last bag?" he asks. "Whatever you say goes."

Stupid men and their ways of settling scores. I'm almost ashamed of being one. I walk over to them, and their grips ease. Turning to the shelf beside them, I reach in with my arm and grab the first thing that I touch. I do this impulsively, without even thinking about it. When I pull my hand back out, a second bag of the same kind of pretzels appears.

"Here," I tell the taller man, tossing the bag at his chest. "Now you can stop arguing over such stupid things as pretzels. There's a world collapsing out there. Do some good with your lives."

Dumbfounded, the two men look at where I just pulled out the bag. They resemble little kids looking inside the hat of a magician, wondering where the rabbit had come from. I roll my cart away from them. Behind me, I can hear the two men apologizing to one another.

After about an hour I manage to find just about everything on my list. I meet Gammy at the line leading to register seven, and after what feels like forever we pay for our groceries and head back out.

Chapter 18

The days roll by slowly, like clouds in the air drifting to the breeze. Each passing second hangs onto my skin like persistent claws that refuse to let go. In some ways it's good that these days take time and time to turn over, becoming part of the past, but sometimes I just wish we could get this done and over with. Including today, only three more days remain in June. Outside, the sun shines its useless light, heatless, still overpowered by the gripping cold that we've all grown so used to.

Ben and I are downtown on Michigan Avenue, window-shopping for useless trinkets like watches, chains, and charms. It's ridiculous to come out here to look at jewelry when in just two days our entire lives will be spun upside down and shaken up like a bad disease, but I feel we need to distract our restless minds. I've gotten so used to my house from being cooped up inside of it that I could tell you where everything is, blindfolded. Today I needed to get out.

The stores and shops are open only because eventually people had to move on with their lives despite the freezing weather. People need to stock up on food and equipment before July, and to do so, money is needed. The whole economic cycle resumed, but at a staggered pace. Inflation boomed on household items and food, then prices dropped and then shot up even higher.

"I'll give you forty for that silver chain," Ben tells the clerk, pointing at the display case on the wall.

"No, no, no," the dark-skinned store owner says with an Indian accent, shaking his head. "That is worth one hundred."

"Fifty," Ben debates firmly.

"Seventy-five," the man offers, quite frustrated. They had been arguing on the price of different items for almost a half hour.

"Shit, man, I don't even want that fucking chain, or anything else in this store."

We walk out as the clerk shouts at us in a language that we cannot understand. Ben laughs and zips up his coat.

"Why did you have to jag him like that?" I ask him, annoyed.

"It was funny." He smiles.

"You shouldn't have wasted his time like that. He probably needs money, and you doing that doesn't help."

"Then *you* buy something," he says, but still in a good humor.

"Can't. I spent all my money helping Gammy pay for our groceries. All the prices leaped, and you wouldn't believe how much food we bought."

"That's what happens when everyone rushes to the store all at once like a bunch of idiots."

"Idiots?" I ask him, offended.

"No, man. I didn't mean it like that. I wasn't trying to call you an idiot." He puts a hand on my shoulder in an apologetic effort.

"Don't tell me you haven't gone out and prepared."

Ben scoffs abruptly. The bright sun bleaches his face, making him look pale. As we keep walking, a scrawny black woman wearing a thin dress and fluffy slippers comes towards us. Her steps are stumbled, as if she were drunk. She passes between us and we turn to observe how little clothes she is wearing for such a cold day.

"Of course we didn't prepare," Ben tells me. "Nothing's actually going to happen! Besides, I've got Jeremy Christ on my side. What could possibly go wrong?"

The black woman sits down on a bench covered in snow. She looks in her thirties, but her face is worn as if her life had pressed twice as many years upon her skin. The crisp powder dissolves, absorbed by her dress. She shivers uncontrollably, embracing herself with her scrawny arms. They tremble frenziedly. Her lower lip vibrates up and down, and as she hums through her clattering teeth, the sound of her voice sounds like an electrified buzz.

Curious, I approach her bench while still talking to Ben. "What do you mean 'you've got me by your side'? Don't you realize that for 40 days I'll be locked inside my house? Do you know what kinds of things will be happening outside?"

"No, what?" he asks apathetically.

"Demons, Ben, will roam the Earth trying to cause as much havoc and terror they can manage." My words come out chillingly, and for a second I see a worried expression on Ben's face, letting me know that I've got his attention.

"What do you mean by 'demons'?" he asks me.

"I mean demons, Ben. *Actual* demons. Satan's army."

"What is this, the end of the world?" His voice sounds dry and lost.

"Yes, actually."

One by one I unsnap the buttons on my coat, and then pull it off my shoulders. "Miss?" I turn to the lady, holding out my coat to her. "Would you like to put this on?"

She doesn't acknowledge me. Instead, she drunkenly reaches for one of her pink slippers and pulls it off. She nearly loses her balance, wobbling unsteadily in her seat. She holds the fluffy shoe in her shivering hands, arms quivering and elbows locked. With one hand she tosses the slipper away onto the street. Seconds later a truck runs over it, turning it a dark, slushy black color.

Her frizzy hair is held up in a scruffy bun, vibrating with the rest of her body and threatening to come loose. Her fingers and knuckles seem to be frozen, each of them locked, making her hands look like twisted paws. Slowly she pulls off the other slipper, fingers struggling to grab hold of it, and throws it on the street, leaving both of her feet bare. Her toes are curled upward, and she holds her legs folded one over the other, crossing at the ankles. The shakes bring her knees to knock against one another.

Awkwardly, she stands up. Her left foot buckles beneath her, and she almost tumbles to the ground. She stumbles for balance for a long moment and then manages to hold herself up with her arms spread to the sides.

"What the hell is she doing?" Ben asks from behind me. I ignore him and keep my attention on the woman.

Her toes are still curled as she stands up on the cold ground. She lets her arms fall to her sides, where her frozen knuckles pinch onto the end of her dress. Slowly she rolls up the fabric, crumpling it as she goes, uncovering her white underwear. I grab her by the arms gently, dropping my coat to the ground and try to get her to pay attention to me. "Miss?" I say, unable to find any other suitable words. Why is she doing this?

For a second I think she's going to let the dress fall back to its length, but then she pulls it off completely in a single swoop. Her bare chest glimmers in the daylight, nipples thrusting coldly. Other than her thin layer of underwear, she's completely nude. I back away, not knowing what else to do. Standing there, she reminds me of a leafless tree shaking in the wind.

With her rigid thumbs she pulls on her underwear's elastic, and lets it drop down to her ankles. Behind me, Ben whistles, enjoying the peek show displayed before him. I look up at her, at her milk-chocolate face, not wanting to see. Her blank stare, disaster stricken and pallid, stares through me. It stares past Ben. Past the buildings surrounding us. Past everything of this world. Her irises fill with black senile apprehension. Her thick lips, now turned bluish and waxy, part open only enough to breathe sheets of air through them. Her breath is invisible. It doesn't condensate into the white puffs that my own and Ben's breath assume.

Looking away, I kneel down to reach for my jacket. When I stand back up, I put it around her, covering her naked body. Her blank face doesn't change, and she doesn't move. I hold the coat onto her with my hands. Then, when I think that it might stay on, I let go of it, but instead the coat falls as before, left unnoticed by the young woman.

"Miss, you're going to freeze to death. Please, take my coat," I say firmly, holding the coat out to her once again.

"No," she says, finally showing signs of acknowledgement. "I cannot take it." Her voice is vacant of emotion, barely reaching for the air. I can hear it only because I am so close to her.

"Please," I insist, about to cover her once more. "You can have it…"

She steps closer to me. Her rigid fingers grasp onto my arms at the elbows and she says, "You mustn't let your fears overcome you, Jeremy." Her eyes widen, and her words come out round, full of dangerous resilience. So much emotion and fear escapes through her words as she speaks. Her eyes are wild now, impossible to tame. "Don't be fooled by the sounds and images you know cannot exist. It is more than demons that will roam the Earth. It is the actual presence of Lucifer that will trick men and women to commit arrogant sins. Many lives will be lost, and just as many souls. Do not become one of them, Jeremy. You are a messenger of God. You cannot fall nor surrender. Do not become one of them."

As she's finishing her last phrase, a large construction van loses control over the thick sheets of ice that coat over the road in layers. The driver tugs the wheel in every direction, desperately trying to set his vehicle back on track. Distracted by this, I don't even notice that the woman has let go of me until I see her walk on the street. The tires on the van lock, skidding and grinding on the slick road of ice. The driver honks at the woman, a sound breathing a huff of death into my ears. The rubber screeches, imploring the woman to get out of the way, but she doesn't listen. Calmly, she stands her ground. Her body is rigid, firm, and upright. She looks up at the gray sky with her neck bent all the way back. She sends a short message in the air that I manage to hear despite the terror trying to steal away my attention.

"I have told him," she says.

The van slams against her body, and goes crashing against a street pole, clamping the woman between the hood of the van and the large, metal pole.

"Oh my God!" Ben shouts from behind me. *"Holy shit!"*

The woman's body stiffens like the cadaver that she's become, but then becomes limp again, making her chest fall forwards. She rests on the hood of the van as blood empties out of her cuts. She doesn't die naked, for her blood covers her body almost completely.

Seconds later I hear a rumble explode from around the corner of a building.

Chapter 19

The tragedy of the woman's death doesn't even seep into our minds. I can't even give it a second thought before my attention is redirected somewhere else.

Screams and cheers twisted in their own terror reach out to the farthest corners of the streets. Anger explodes, mouthed by thousands of voices. The screams diffuse among the streets as deranged people carry havoc and destruction without a logical course or plan. Their only goal is shaped by the chaos that they bring forth.

A riot has formed on the streets of Detroit.

It is a single riot shaped by what seems like thousands and thousands of men and women, and it sweeps towards us in a wave of catechistic hate. Almost everyone is armed, if only equipped by their own rage, and willing to use whatever weapon they have in hand. Instantly I feel petrified, like a man with his legs cemented to the ground.

Hate shapes their faces into unmistakable grimaces. Their mouths spread open and shut in turns, screaming through their teeth. Screaming their rage. Screaming their shouts at us as if they were spears. It's as if their shrieks alone could kill. Their eyebrows are locked down to the top of their noses in a downward slope.

Approaching the intersection crossing Michigan Avenue and Washington Boulevard, the crowd spreads in around us from three different fronts. My heart pounds at a tambourine's rate, begging me to run.

They are coming for me. Something tells me this, and I believe it. Their faces lock down on me like sunlight narrowing into a hot ray of light through a magnifying glass. The crowd lunges towards us, insistent with hate.

A group of three men surround a trash bin that seems buckled to the ground. They rock it back and forth, the hinges and bolts coming loose. In normal circumstances, it would have taken them all day and all night for them to even shake it loose, but not even a minute later, the trashcan is stripped completely from its bolts. A large gorilla of a man grabs the trashcan and starts running with the rest of the crown. He bends his body backwards like a catapult drawing back to be loaded. His arms thrust forward, and his grip lets go of the metal can. In midair, trash disperses from its container, falling to the ground like filthy confetti. The can shoots through the air at eye-blinking speed, hurling to clobber me across the chest. Instinctively, I drop to the ground to dodge the can's wrath, and the metal barrel crashes through the windshield of a small car parked behind me.

As the windshield shatters, shards of glass explode outward like thousands of uncut diamonds. Some hit my back, but my coat, which fortunately I had slipped back on, protects me from any cuts.

I turn to Ben and ask, "Are you okay?"

The left side of his face is filled with jagged cuts that cross diagonally on his skin. Little drops of blood trickle out, and the corner of his lip is gashed badly. He spits out blood, along with a single sliver of glass that tings onto the ground. He says nothing.

"Run!" I scream, incapable of saying anything more. Willingly, he does so, and together we bolt on the slippery sidewalk. Patches of smooth ice are scattered everywhere on the ground, hidden like mines under the snow, making it impossible to move very fast. After every few steps, one of us nearly slips and glides for half a second.

Ben quickly dodges to the right, trying to avoid collision with a storekeeper who's just stepped outside to take a look at all the noise. Dodging the door, Ben runs through a tall pile of snow. As the snow spread out from the pile, a fire hydrant beneath is revealed. His legs buckle against the metal stump, and his body thrusts forward, doing a half spin in midair. Instantly, a large pick-up truck appears on the street, slamming right into him, hurling Ben sideways. The driver hits the breaks after slamming against Ben's body, but the tires slide uncontrollably. The body of the vehicle spins around, doing a hundred-and-eighty-degree turn. The back bumper plows a row of rioters, knocking them down like human bowling pins. Then the massive tires of the truck roll over them, crushing their bodies underneath.

Ben's body lies on the ground limply.

Still gliding on ice, I grab hold of the nearest parked car to stop myself, almost slipping and falling to the ground. I run to Ben, putting my arms around his torso to help him up. My grip loosens, though, when I take a look at his legs.

A sharp bone cuts out of his left shin, slicing through the cloth of his pants like a shark fin out of water. His other leg is bent completely backwards at the knee, agonizingly opposite of the way it should look like. A quick squirt of blood spits out of his left leg, but then the pressure beneath settles and the red liquid flows out like a stream, lapping over his pants.

I scream, shrieking for Ben's pain, but then my voice is devoured by the massive shouts of the rioters. I grab Ben's limp body in my arms, facing him towards me, hoping to shake life back in his limbs.

"Ben!" I scream at his face, searching desperately for a response. His eyelids flicker, but his pupils have slipped back into a dark unconscious. Above his right eye, a wide cut spreads his skin apart, revealing a gnarled sliver of his skull. He breathes inward once. The breath comes in as a heavy gulp of air, and as he tries to exhale, a gasp creaks in his throat like a rusty hinge rubbing against wood. A slobbered, gagging sound chokes in his throat as if he were gargling petroleum. A drop of saliva spits out, settling on his bottom lip.

The world stops turning in that moment, holding its breath and bracing.

Ben dies in my arms.

All around, angry men and women close in without remorse. I stand up, leaving Ben on the cold ground, and face the crowd that surrounds me. Sticks, bats, and anger are their weapons, and they're just waiting for the right moment to use them.

A scrawny teenager with his clothes and coat half torn to shreds crouches on top of a phone booth. Patches of cloth dangle from the sides of his trench coat. White powder is smudged over his face along with strokes of black ink painting his lips and contouring his eyes. He holds a hollow metal pipe and points it at me. He's directing the crowd from on top of the booth. A queer smile forms on his lips, snarling the grimace of a rabid animal. I recognize him. He's that satanic teenager I beat up on the school parking lot back in April.

He shouts to the crowd, which seems to be obeying his every word, and the people circle around me, tightening closer and closer.

"Jeremy!" the lunatic yells from above. "You remember me?"

It takes me a moment to remember his name. "Tyler Crandall," I say out loud, shouting it with disgust.

"That's right." His sadistic grin widens, and his eyes blaze with lunacy. The crowd stops its advance, commanded by a single gesture from Tyler's hand. How can so many people be following and listening to one person's commands? Especially to a young teenager? Whatever happened to the mob psychology?

The faces of those surrounding me become blank. Their eyes are hollow, like holes burrowed into a tree deep enough to reach its interior darkness. And yet, beyond their facial blanks, anger is still visible on the surface, steaming with artificial rage. All of this seems to come from within. Their anger is unjustified and misplaced over their faces. It's as if it's been injected into their blood stream by some outer force that shouldn't be meddling with their minds.

The crowd quiets a little, emitting only slow murmurs that don't exceed whispers. Tyler begins to speak again. "Do you remember what I told you months ago, when we first met? I predicted that Lucifer would have control of this Earth. And look at this now. Look around you, Jeremy. We're two days away from the infamous Judgment, and already I'm in command of an army of thousands. All these souls have submitted themselves to our King. King Lucifer will reign all.

"Don't you see?" he continues. "There is no hope left. There is no love. There is no God willing to save you from this. You've been defeated before you could even begin to fight, and *this*, this full throttled army of destruction, is your proof."

He sounds like an actor being fed a script of lines, his voice reaching just beyond a self-contained madness. Above everyone, on top of the telephone booth, he commands his brainwashed followers. He stands as the general of this army of darkness.

Dense clouds form in the sky, turning everything gray and colorless beneath. The aged and dreary looking buildings around us add to the detached feeling of the crowd. Even the high-reaching sky scrapers slowly transform into dark towers held in their own monstrosity.

"This is it!" Tyler exclaims. "This is the moment when the direct messenger of God dies. You've done your job, and so you've become useless now. You have no purpose left on this Earth, and I'll take full responsibility for your death, Jeremy. King Lucifer will reward me for this. I'll become His right hand."

He talks as if he's just signed a contract with his worshiped Satan, granting his entrance to his own version of paradise.

Tyler roars a scream into the frozen air, signaling his army to do their job. Their morbidly detached faces close in on me. They begin to shout and scream as before. What they say is not important. What they scream is mostly shrills of dread that have no intended context in words.

The clouds roll over atop one another in the sky, pressing together into a dense ceiling of pallid billow. Then the spread of clouds becomes so thick that no sunlight can seep through. There are no holes, gaps or errors in that impossibly thick ceiling. It becomes solid throughout.

The shade of early dawn falls over the streets. No color exists. The zombified men and women take slow, paced steps to approach me. They know that I have no escape.

Finally, the same man who had flung the trashcan earlier swoops a meaty arm down, hooking my legs. Then both arms come around, clamping my knees tightly, making them crack against one another. More and more of them jump on me, pushing me down on the ground. Terrifying expressions fill my vision, filling every gap as the clouds did with the sky.

A scrawny woman with short brown hair scratches at my face with her bony fingers, trying to rip my skin from my cheeks and jaws. A set of dull teeth bites down on my calf. I'm being pulled in so many different directions that it feels like my bones will pop out of their joints, and then my skin will tear off with them. My left arm is ragged and twisted backwards, ready to snap like a chicken bone if only pulled harder.

I cough up a nasty explosion of air, and spit splatters outward, landing on the scrawny woman's face. She doesn't care. She only digs deeper into my cheeks.

All I can feel is pain.

Burns and fleshy flames of pain lick my body in abrasive tongue flicks, reaching out to the deepest of degrees. Pain always feels like a burn, I've noticed. It could be a cut, a smashed finger, a slap in the face or even humiliation in front of a crowd. It doesn't matter which. Pain is pain, and no matter what form it decides to take, it always feels like flames scarring flesh. This is what hell must be like. This is why hell is always represented by gigantic flames scalding everything from surface to ceiling.

A burly round knee impacts against my chest. I cough again, but this time, instead of saliva, I spit up a string of black blood. It's as black as a jet of oil, without light to give it color for the eye to see.

There is no hope.

There is no love.

From somewhere, a group of hands turn me over. My chin smacks the ground. Then my head is yanked back by my hair, neck curving like a strained arch, just waiting and praying to be snapped off. Then, down my face goes, smacking on the icy and impossibly hard ground. The skin just above my eyebrows splits open and blood clods over my eyes.

Suddenly, like the last sturdy leg of a table cracking, my acceptance for this pain collapses.

No more!

Without a single premeditated thought, my mouth bursts open and I shout, "God, my Lord! My Savior! Help me!" In that instant, a surge of energy runs through my body like a blast of electricity. I spring to my hands and knees, pushing everyone off of my body. Slowly, I step to my feet.

A huge, round hole opens up in the thick ceiling of clouds right above my head. For an instant, it's like looking into a black hole that leads into an infinite nowhere. A moment passes, and then light gathers inside of it, forming a pure white circle amidst the dirty mesh of gray.

The light burns down upon me from above, forming a huge beam of energy shaped by the hole that it comes from. Those circling me incinerate at the first touch of light. They glow white for an instant before they finally turn to ashes. Deep burns tare layers of skin and muscle tissue away from their faces and bodies.

Tyler is flung out from his high position, and falls somewhere among the sea of heads. They all attempt to run away, clawing and pushing each other aside to get through, doing whatever they can to escape the beam of light that blankets over me. Seconds pass and the white beam fades away, but I feel my body still filled with its surge. The light having disappeared, they turn back to me, scheming, snarling, dreading, but before they have a chance to attack, my voice explodes from my lips in grenade fragments.

I feel sucked inward for an instant, almost imploding from deep within my chest, but then it all explodes outward. A potent energy spreads out like a huge ball of flames, spreading in every direction like an atomic bomb stretching into a nuclear disaster. Intensive flurries of heat follow, expanding the air with such extremity that it crushes everything in its path to smithereens. I can actually see the air around me morphing, rolling, stretching, as if it were transparent rubber instead.

Cars and other vehicles are pushed back against buildings and flattened by the high pressure. All the windows burst, and a few of the buildings collapse, crumbling to the ground. The roaring sound that engulfs everything is tremendous. It's like being in the heart of a tornado.

The rioters are smothered by the heat and liquefied instantly. Their faces melt and then vaporize. Thousands of men and women, who just seconds ago were trying to rip me apart, vanish completely, replaced by massive mounds of ash and unrecognizable body parts lying everywhere on the ground.

The smell of spoiled meat and burnt hair fills the air, trapped in by the clouds still above. I gag, unable to help myself, followed by a long stream of vomit. Looking down on me, my clothes are stained in maroon patches of dried blood and smudges of black ash. Finally, the clouds begin to roll away and fade. This happens slowly, like foamy waves on shore returning back to their ocean.

I remain as the only survivor. A few feet away, Ben's body is the only one that has remained intact. I look down at him, wondering how and why he hasn't been incinerated with the rest.

I study him with curiosity for a minute. His legs are still broken. His body is still limp. His face is still lifeless. And yet he has not been vaporized.

I realize then why, and I know how hard it will be to do what I have to.

Chapter 20

Coming downtown, I had parked my car at a gas station. When the blast of white light exploded, it spread out to a radius of few blocks wide. Buildings became bleached on the sides facing me. Parked cars and other vehicles have been crushed like compacted clown cars. Windows across buildings and stores have been wiped hollow, glass having turned back to sand or broken into infinite shards.

I remember now how far I had parked the car when coming downtown just to avoid paying for parking. Maybe there, at least it's still intact. I crouch down beside Ben and drag his twisted body until his knee caps lock. It's almost impossible because his one knee is snapped back in the opposite direction. I try to stand him up. His balance is wobbly and keeps buckling under, but then finally I'm able to kneel beside him and place his torso over my shoulder. I walk towards the direction of my car, stopping every few blocks to ease the ache on my shoulder. My knees buckle every few steps, and my calf still burns with rays of pain. Once outside the radius of the blast, I switch shoulders and continue to trudge along.

No breeze fills the air, holding its breath for the tragedy lying just behind me. A traffic sign turns green, but there are no cars to drive through it. To my right, about ten stories high, a car has crashed against a building so that the bottom of it faces outward. One of the tires is still spinning, wobbling really, on its bent axle. Out here, instead of ashes, piles of crushed bodies and missing limbs layer the narrow sidewalks. The air smells like vanilla extract drenching over piles and piles of butchered meat covered in flies. Just to walk through the streets I have to step in between crumbled ruins, junkyard cars, and the occasional body sprawled across the way.

When I finally reach my car, a boxy 1988 Civic, I notice that most of the windshield is cracked and that the headlights have burst. Despite that, the car is in drivable condition and mostly intact.

I open the passenger door and carefully lower Ben's body into his seat. I sit at the wheel and turn the ignition. I drive out of the gas station's parking lot, and for just a moment I'm filled with a terrible apathy, destroying any urge to go on. I just want to die. I just want to drive my car at 90 miles an hour into the next building I can crash into.

But then I draw back.

That would be cowardly. That would be the ultimate act of weakness. By committing suicide I would be escaping whatever responsibilities and duties God has planned for me.

I couldn't die in such a cowardly manner. I have to be strong—the ultimate, cliché statement, but it's the only true one I can think of for now. I keep driving, determined that I'll stay alive.

Minutes later, sirens blare onto the streets, all heading towards the destruction site I've created. Police cars speed out without stopping, followed by a row of ambulances. They'll be lucky if they find anyone to save.

Reaching Ben's house, I park the car in front of his driveway, letting the engine idle. I breathe in and out deeply for a minute or so, giving me the time to gather enough courage and strength to do what I have to. This must be the hardest thing in my life.

No, that's stupid.

The hardest thing was watching my parents die, but this is up there along with it.

I stare at Ben's house through my cracked window. The sky behind it frowns, stricken with contrasting swirls of black and gray clouds. Looking at it through the scattered cracks, the house itself looks shattered. Just like everything else in my life.

An aura of sadness surrounds the house, as if it were expecting my arrival and the news I had to bring. The streets are silent. The only noise I can hear is the rumble of my engine. A tear plops out my eye and strolls down my face. Then another follows, racing the first to the bottom. I turn off the car and the engine shuts off, leaving me soundless in my solitude.

I look at Ben one more time. His head is leaned back on the seat, his mouth and eyes still open. I shut his eyes with the palm of my hand gently, unable to bear their look. I take a deep breath, stilling everything in my mind.

More tears fall to my lips, allowing me to taste their dread.

I can't do this, I tell myself. But I know that I have to. And I know that I will.

I step out and reach Ben's side of the car. I pull him out gently and pick him up in my arms. He's heavy, but I put the thought away for now, knowing that it isn't important. Holding him out in both arms feels like the only way to present him to his parents. It's the best way—if there is such a thing in the presenting of a dead son to a mother and father.

My footsteps carry me closer and closer to the door. I wipe my tears off onto my shoulder, but I can still feel my eyes glossed over. I try to hold back the tears, knowing that I shouldn't.

I fumble around with Ben, lowering my torso, and I manage to ring the doorbell with my thumb. A few seconds pass. The seconds feel like minutes, hours, days, months. They feel infinite, but then the door finally opens. A large man with a square face and a tidy haircut fills the doorway.

Silence.

Just dreary silence. What do you say to the father of your dead best friend? His mouth opens, attempting to gasp, to say something, to scream maybe, but it finds itself breathless. His eyes are wide and shocked.

"Mr. Norton…" I say. Nothing comes next.

How do you finish such a sentence when this is what you have to offer? He doesn't speak. I don't speak.

Silence.

Suddenly, I feel so awkward and ashamed. Here I am, facing a man who's lost his son, and all I can do is look up at him with Ben in my arms.

Finally he takes him from me. Some of that awkwardness fades, but my shame doesn't. He sobs, hugging and grasping Ben tightly with his feet dangling.

"This is so hard," I say softly as if to justify my inability to speak.

A short, stout woman with short black hair approaches the doorway, asking, "Dear, what's wrong?"

Mrs. Norton sees her husband holding their son. Her face freezes. Her expression is of deep, dug-up sorrow that can't be found anywhere else other than at the footsteps of this house.

Ben is dead, I want to say. *There was a mob, a truck, confusion, and it all happened in an instant. It all happened so fast.* Disasters always seem to happen "so fast." There never seems any other way to describe them.

Her face turns to me, and her expression turns into anger. It turns into rage. It is the essence of fury, forming an unspoken accusation. I can hear her words coming out before she even speaks them.

"What did you do?" she screams at me. In the eyes of a mother, it's always the bearer of bad news who's responsible for what happened.

"What did you do to my son?" she repeats, screaming louder. She shrieks, forming hysteria in her voice. I say nothing. I have no reputable answer to her accusing question. I am already guilty in her eyes. There's nothing I can say that will take that away.

She tries to lunge for me, wanting to rip my face apart even more than the woman in the riot already has.

"Katrina," her husband calls for her. Ultimately, Mr. Norton drops his son to the ground to grab a hold of his wife. He holds her back. She is still screaming and crying. Her face depicts every form of detest. She hates me. There's nothing that will take that away.

In her eyes I am the one responsible for her son's death.

Don't shoot the messenger doesn't apply to this woman.

"Katrina," Ben's father repeats, trying to calm his wife down. He, just like me, is at a loss of words.

She keeps screaming.

He keeps repeating her name.

I keep silent without defending myself in any way.

"Go home," Ben's father tells me as gently as he can possibly manage. My head falls. I take a step back and I turn away.

Chapter 21

I don't go home immediately. For about an hour or so I drive aimlessly with the only purpose of thinking things through. Once I finally get home, I enter the house silently. The door clicks behind me, cutting off the cold wind. I take off my coat and let it fall in the closet.

Gammy is on the couch reading a novel. "How's it going?" she asks. As if there's any possible way of answering that question. I keep silent. It's the only thing I can do.

She marks her page with a bookmark and stands up. "Jeremy, what's the matter?" Then she takes a look at me, noticing my torn face and stained clothes. "Oh my goodness! What happened? What did you do to yourself!"

"Everyone is dead," I answer emotionlessly. She looks confused, not understanding. I don't expect her to.

"What do you mean?"

There is no way of explaining any of it. A woman threw herself in front of a van, Ben collided against an oncoming truck, and over a thousand people disintegrated before my eyes. How do you begin? How do you possible express any of it into words?

"I mean exactly that: everyone is dead." And maybe, by that I also mean that everyone else in the world is bound to die, and therefore we're all as good as dead. It's all useless, like chasing after the wind.

Gammy's expression doesn't change. Her lips are parted, the gap between them no thicker than a hair, and her eyes slant down with confound worry.

The phone rings once. Seconds pass and then it rings again. I pick it up and hold it to my ear.

"Hello?" I ask.

"Hi," a deep, lifeless voice says absently. "Jeremy?" It's Ben's father.
"Yes, it's me, Mr. Norton."

"Good, I wanted to talk to you." Silence follows. The voice sighs into my ear before deciding to go on. "When I opened the door today, there wasn't anything that I expected less to find than you holding my dead son in your arms. I was shocked. I was speechless. I didn't know how to react. In my head I had so many questions to ask, but I couldn't manage to word any of them out. I don't suppose now I feel any different." He sounds like he has been crying. I don't blame him. His words come through thinly. It's hard to hear him speak over the phone. I can tell from his voice that he's desperately trying to hold himself back from bursting out into cries. He should be crying. He shouldn't be holding anything back.

In the background I can hear Ben's mother shrieking tears at the top of her lungs, every wail audible. "My wife Katrina, is still very shaken, you understand. She was angry, and in a way so was I. It took me a while to settle her down, but I don't believe it did either of us any good. She's started up again, as you can hear. Still, more and more questions formed, and I just don't know where to begin, Jeremy. I guess what I want to ask is this: how did it happen? How did my son die?"

His questions sound as if he's holding back on what he's really trying to ask me. In some way it sounds as if what he really wants to know is: how could I have *let* it happen?

Guilt cringes at my jawbone and forces my eyes to water. I had managed to save myself from that deranged crowd, but how come I hadn't been able to do the same for Ben?

It takes me a second to form the right words to answer him. Slowly I begin to explain what happened. Little by little my voice trebles more as I speak. I tell him about us shopping downtown. Then I tell him how the riot formed, chasing us away. Finally my words are impossible to understand, mixed in with broken down sobs. I gulp back, and I finally try to explain how Ben smashed into the incoming truck headfirst. "He died moments later in my arms," I say, as if that detail were incredibly important.

"What happened after that?" he asks, knowing that the story isn't complete.

"After that…I brought Ben's body to you, Mr. Norton," I say, evading his question. I know exactly what he's asking. He wants to know how I could've possibly survived the mob when his son didn't.

"No, I mean after Ben died. How did you escape? You said that you were trapped. You were surrounded by hundreds, maybe thousands of people. So how did you get away?"

"I'm afraid I don't know how to answer that question, Mr. Norton. Even if I did, you wouldn't believe me."

I know that not answering his question isn't fair to him. His son is dead. He deserves to know the rest of the story. But what would it change? How could I even make him understand? He would call me a liar. He would think I was crazy.

"Weird things have been happening lately, Mr. Norton," I tell him, "and what happened next was just one more on top of the rest. It was something incomprehensible. Watch the news tonight. I'm sure you'll get the answer you're looking for there, but I still don't think you'll believe it. I'm sorry that Ben died. There's nothing I could've done."

Over the phone I can hear him crying.

"Before you hang up," I say over his sobs, "do me a favor. Please prepare for what's about to happen. Please go out and buy what you need to last you and your wife for forty days. This is nothing to blow over, Mr. Norton. I'll pray for you."

He hangs up and the cries cut off. All I can hope is that he heard me and that he'll listen to my advice.

About a half hour later, the doorbell rings. I open it and see a police officer standing at the doorway.

"Can I help you?" I ask.

"Jeremy Christ, right?"

"Yeah, that's me."

"Hi, I'm Officer Barrera. I just finished talking with Mr. and Mrs. Norton and I suggested to them that I'd come over your house to understand things better."

"Sure, come in."

"Thank you, this is only going to take a few minutes. Just to let you know, you're not being charged with the death of Mr. and Mrs. Norton's son, Benjamin. This is just to help me fill out my report."

"I understand."

"Can you tell me what happened?" he says, pulling out a metal block pad.

"I've already told Ben's dad the whole story."

"I know, but for the record I need you to tell me about it because you were there, and not Mr. Norton. Is there anything that happened that you didn't tell him about?"

"Well, Ben and I were downtown—"

"Downtown? This was today?" he asks, taken aback.

"Yeah, that's right. We were shopping at some of the stores."

"The reason I'm asking is that I came from downtown just before Mr. Norton called about the death of his son. The place was destroyed—it was—" he stammers, trying to find the words to describe it.

"I know. I was there when it happened."

"You were there?" he says incredulously.

"I was the one who caused it."

Chapter 22

The last Sunday morning of June has finally approached. Gammy and I enter St. Regis, and I'm not at all shocked to see the entire place packed with people, all wearing neckties or dresses. Every possible seat is occupied and there are even more people standing, pressed against one another, pushing against the walls.

I remember how I felt coming here months ago, back in April. My skin had crept with itching, and my bones must have squeaked walking up this same aisle. Walking inside this church had felt like walking in deep mud, uneasy and trudging. And even though the place hasn't changed since April, as I'm looking at it again, it seems brighter and more colorful. The people seem warmer. The paintings and statues could be breathing right now. The choir rehearsing their tunes sounds like it's warming up for an opera rather than about to perform for a few hundred churchgoers.

A jubilant murmur spreads through the people. My face is still badly cut, but that's not what the murmurs are taking notice of. They are all so happy to see me. Smiles, and laughter, and people clasping hands are all that I see and hear. As we keep walking, people stand to offer us their seats. Small children run for me, begging to be hugged, offering drawings, and asking to be picked up. Men and women shake my hand as a receiving of blessing. They all tell me how happy they are to see me and how glad they are that I've come. Some embrace me without a forewarning word, hugging so tightly that my lungs clasp breathlessly. Others start crying before I can even get close to them. The joy is so vivid in this church that it seems to hold a life of its own.

In a way, I feel like a fraud here, though. They're all begging to touch me and for me to speak to them, but what they don't know is that just yesterday I was responsible for the oblivion of over a thousand men and women. They don't know who I really am inside, or about all the innumerable times I've held up a beer to the chants of "Chug! Chug! Chug!" They come to me in search of spiritual satisfaction, but in all honesty, I don't know how much of that I can provide. I'm no better than any of them, and actually I feel inferior to them. Up until a month ago I didn't even accept God's existence, while some of these people have welcomed Him in their lives probably since they were little. It's at times like this that I don't understand why God chose me. Me, out of all of these people.

"Jeremy! Mrs. Christ! So glad you came," Father Birmingham says to us warmly from beside the entrance. "Come," he says, waving us towards him. He greets us with a wide grin, and his face ripples back with a smile, unveiling with delight. Behind his round glasses, his eyes spark with cheer. A long golden robe falls from his shoulders. A white dove is embroidered on the front with an olive twig in its beak. He shakes my hands with two of his own. He leans closer to me and asks, "Can I ask you something?"

"Sure," I say.

"Well, I was wondering if you could speak for us today at the end of Mass. I would greatly appreciate a few words from you, maybe to encourage and strengthen our souls. I know that half of the people attending today feel so very lost, and it would be reassuring if you could wish us a brief farewell."

"I would love to," I answer, surprising myself. What? Did I just say that? What am I going to say to these people? I open my mouth to withdraw my acceptance, but it's too late.

"Great. We've reserved you two seats in the first row. Go ahead and sit. We're about to begin."

"They're so happy to see you," Gammy whispers in my ear proudly, as she gives my hand a soft squeeze.

"I'm happy to see *them*," I admit, stunned. "But I don't know what to tell them. The next forty days may depend entirely on what I say to them."

"Say what is in your heart."

"And what would that be?" I say, my face twisted unsurely.

"Say what you feel right now, and tell it the way you feel it. *That* is what is in your heart." She presses her palm on the center of my chest, and a warm flood oozes through me like liquid. She offers a warm smile and then turns her attention to the priest as he begins Mass. As Father Birmingham speaks, I find myself completely enveloped by his words. He speaks glamorously, explaining God's will for us, His people.

He tells us anecdotes from his past, mentioning my father who had been there during the roughest part of his life. In an hour's worth of time, he packs so much love, so much faith, so much self-imposed strength that I can't help but feel it within me. Like a donation freely accepted. Like a transfusion of sacred blood, only through words. Like a connection of souls.

Finally, as he finishes Mass, he gives a quick introduction of me to the crowd. The entire church explodes in a round of applause and cheers, and Father John gestures me to the microphone.

He steps aside as I take his position and the crowd goes on clapping. A group of teens cheers my name, while others whistle in good humor.

"Thanks," I say over the mike, blushing.

My palms are dampened by sweat, and I'm still not sure of what I'm going to say. I take advantage of the crowd's cheers, waiting for them to quiet down so that I can find the right words to speak.

"God works in mysterious ways," I finally begin once the crowd has become silent. "How many of you have heard that one before? I know I have more than a few times, especially after losing my parents. I *hated* hearing that phrase. I wanted to rip those words to shreds every time I saw them on a greeting card. Every day it was, 'God's mysterious ways, God's mysterious ways,' over and over again. It lost meaning after hearing it so much. It didn't seem to answer anything. Not one bit. I couldn't stand the fact that God had mysteries and was keeping secrets. Why were there so many of them? And why always so confusing? Yet, sometimes it's the mystery part that we enjoy most. It's the not knowing that satisfies us, and being able to leave it at that.

"Sometimes, when faced with a mystery, we tell ourselves, 'No, but I really want to know *why!* Or *how!*' But then, once the truth comes out, revealing the mystery, we draw back and do everything to escape it. It is *then*, once we know what we had wanted to know for so long, that we try to take it all back. But we can't.

"At first I was oblivious to why God had chosen *me* to reveal that shocking message in this church. I kept asking myself, 'Why this? Why that?' Then slowly, I began to understand that God chose me because I am important to him. He chose me, because he *loves* me. *Me!* Jeremy Christ! An 18-year-old constant sinner who, up until recently, completely denied God's very existence. Out of billions of people I drew the short straw. It took me a while to understand it, and even longer to accept it. But now I've become comfortable with the knowledge. I'm happy to know that God loves me because there's no greater feeling beside it.

"But don't think that I am in any way more special in God's eyes than any of you. My grandma, who means the world to me, told me not long ago that God loves each of us individually, and all equally. That meant a lot to me then and even more so now that I can appreciate those words for their truth. So you see, you shouldn't turn to me for strength and guidance. Turn to yourselves. Or better yet, turn to God! Building a close relationship with Him is the *only* way to survive what's ahead of us.

"Honestly, there's nothing greater than—"

Suddenly my speech is interrupted, not by the crowd cheering, but by the doors to the church's entrance crashing against the walls with a bang. All the heads in the church turn, gasping. There, at the entryway, a short woman wearing an opened bathrobe and baggy pajamas stands clutching a double-barreled shotgun.

I've seen that shotgun countless of times before, mounted on the wall of Mr. Norton's studio along with a collection of others. That sleek piece was his prized possession because it was the first gun he'd ever shot. Every time I went over Ben's house, Mr. Norton would tell me how he'd fractured his breast bone and threw out his shoulder shooting that gun when he was nine. And every time I would listen, giving the gun a glimpse, nodding and smiling at each cue.

Looking at that double barrel now brings everything but a smile.

The entire crowd drops to the ground, screaming, praying, crying. Mrs. Norton scans the scene with the end of her barrel. Her short black hair is messy, sprawling in all directions with a static effect. Even from up at the altar I can see the deep, dark bags under her eyes. A heavy handbag hangs from her shoulder, filled to the brim with shotgun shells. There's enough ammo in her bag to kill everyone here a thousand times over.

Once, Mr. Norton had showed me what was inside his armoire. He unlocked the wooden doors, revealing stacks and stacks of shotgun shells.

"Why so much ammo?" I had asked him, more curious than terrified at the time.

"Because you never know when the world's coming to an end," he had said.

Mrs. Norton gives out the pained shriek of a madwoman. "Jeremy!" she screams, as she points the end of her gun straight for my face. "You killed my son!" A blast from the barrel shoots out, exploding into hundreds of pellets. Her body jerks back at the blast, but she holds her balance. This isn't the first time she's shot that weapon. I duck before the blast can tear my face off, and the huge wooden crucifix comes tumbling down from behind me. I roll out of its way, and it crashes to the ground, cracking in several pieces. Everyone—the priest, Gammy and the young altar boys—has long hit the ground by now, covering their heads with their hands.

Katrina, the maniac that she's become since the loss of her son, screams, "Goddamnit!" Her barrel clicks open. Swiftly, she pops in two more shells, and clacks the huge gun back into firing position.

Having jumped out from behind the podium, I remain exposed. I'm a free-for-all target to the woman in the opened bathrobe. I lunge behind a thick wooden bench. Katrina fires again, and an explosion of wooden splinters shoots jagged chips everywhere. All around, children are crying, women are screaming, and men are hovering over both, covering them as shields.

Mrs. Norton runs up the aisle. Her bare-naked feet thump on the carpet as shells fall from her bag, bouncing off the patted ground.

Click. Reload. Relock.

The three motions sound mechanically produced. Her hands don't even quiver. Her hands are like machines of their own—the only part of her still tamed and kept under control.

I crouch around, trying to conceal myself behind any possible bench, but at the same time trying to avoid endangering others. That's almost impossible. There are people everywhere. Confusion arches all around until it's so thick that the ceiling should be crumbling from it. My eyes poke above my concealment, trying to find Mrs. Norton. She stands beside the broken crucifix, looking around in search of me, keeping the gun pointed wherever she turns. People begin to spread to the closest fire exits, screaming and crying, but there are so many of them that the process seems endless. They press and push one another out of panic, making the escape even more agonizing.

Then, as the crowd spreads out, the bench in front of me is knocked over, leaving me exposed. It takes Katrina a second to see me, but then she jerks the gun quickly, aiming deadly like a hawk snapping its head to hone down its prey.

The closest thing that can hide me again is the huge organ with its tall metal pipes coming up from the top. I run towards it, keeping my body low to the ground, my knees actually hitting my chest. The tip of her shotgun traces after me. She fires again. One of the tiny pellets penetrates my torso and a rose of pain blooms, petals turning to fish hooks under my left rib. The rest of the blast tears away a chunk of the confessional. She screams again, enraged for having missed me for the second time.

Click. Reload. Relock.

Once again, the three sounds come through so automatically that it's frightening. Her only objective is to take me down. Nothing else is on her mind. She's plagued by this fixation.

Below my rib a small patch of blood pours out to stain my shirt. My wounds just keep piling up, and I wonder how many more there are still yet to come. I press my back to the organ, panting heavily and breathing hard. Breathing—as if you could call it that. It's more like grasping for the last wisp of air that I may ever get to draw in.

It takes me a few seconds to realize how I can end all of this. Knowing well the risks, I take a chance anyway. I poke my head out from the side of the organ, begging and hoping that she'll shoot. The gun jerks to make the final adjustment, aligning with my head.

The gun fires. I pull my head back just in time, and the side of the organ explodes. Awful tunes erupt from the pipes, sounding like bullhorns in distress.

This is my chance.

I rush out from behind the organ, charging at full speed towards Mrs. Norton.

Click—her barrel opens.

I run faster and faster, and yet everything's in slow motion. As I'm running, each passing split second spans out like a paper fan, allowing me to view every frame individually. Katrina's face is knotted in hate. The people keep spreading towards the exits. Most of the men, women, and children are rushing out the doors while the rest are still down, holding themselves and each other on the ground.

Katrina's hand grabs two more shells from her bag. Not a twitch stirs her fingers. She clutches them tightly, and then shoves them into the metal tubes. The two shells tick inside their fittings.

Reload.

I'm a flash of a second away from her. I leap off the ground with all my body thrusting forward. Her wrists flick, twisting disgracefully. The barrel snaps into place.

Relock.

Her finger braces the trigger, but then my shoulder impacts against her chest, knocking her to the ground. The gun flies out of her hands, spinning and twisting. The rifle then lands a few feet away from a man covering his two children. The gun doesn't shoot. It doesn't burst or explode. It just hits the ground, and then tumbles around to a stop.

By then I have the mentally deranged woman pinned to the ground, but not easily so. By now she's kicking, twisting, buckling, screaming, doing everything to try to get me off of her. I struggle with her, trying to hold her arms away from me.

"Grab that gun," I tell the man closest to it. The man looks up, shifting his eyes to the weapon. He crawls over to it and grabs it. The man stands up, pointing the gun at Mrs. Norton, trembling in his arms. That man never thought that he'd be holding a gun today.

God does work in mysterious ways.

"Drop the weapon!" sharp voices scream from the entrance. I look back and see a group of SWAT officers blocking the doorway, holding sniper rifles and pistols. By now the cry of a woman running through the streets holding a shotgun must have reached them, and they've come just in time.

The man holding the gun turns to them confused. His grip loosens and the gun rolls out of his fingers. The shotgun falls to the ground, bouncing once, then twice, and then stops. Katrina pushes me off of her and leaps to her weapon. She fumbles with it as she stands up. I look up to see the end of the barrel inches away from my face.

A bombardment of shots from the police rushes towards her. She falls backwards squeezing the trigger and shoots a hole the size of the moon into the ceiling.

She dies with her blood blending into the maroon carpeted floors.

Chapter 23

How can you sleep after that? How do you even fool yourself in closing your eyes in the darkness? Slowly, after endless hours of my eyes drying themselves to round rocks, after hours and hours of plagued thoughts and mindless terrors, morning finally comes. I stay in bed until light eventually decides to haze down through the window just above my head.

The electronic clock on my radio tells me it's just three minutes past six in big numbers formed by green flashy lines. I get out of bed, unrested, muscles creaking as if they were stiffened to my bones, and I start my regular routine: get clothed, brush my teeth, shave, and the sort.

In the living room, Gammy sits on the couch watching the morning news. In her hands she holds a big mug of coffee. She sips on it slowly, pressing her lips to the rim, and then gives me a smile.

"Good morning," she says.

"Morning, Gammy. You couldn't sleep either, huh?"

"Not even a wink. Are you going to shovel the driveway? It's been days since you last did."

"I wasn't planning on it, but I can if you want me to."

"Thank you," she says smiling.

From the closet I gather what I need to dress warm: my coat, gloves, hat and whatnot. I slip everything on snugly and grab the snow shovel that's resting against the wall beside the front door. With the doorknob in one hand and the shovel in the other, I swing the door open and step out.

I freeze, although ironically that isn't the right word to describe it. I stop at the entrance facing outside, and I become motionless. I drop the shovel and the wooden handle clunks to the ground.

"Gammy?" I shout for her, not taking my eyes away from my view.

"Yes, Jeremy?"

"Come here and look at this, quick."

"What is it?"

"You need to see this, I swear."

"Don't swear," she says jokingly. From behind me, I hear her setting the mug down on the glass coffee table and her slippers swish-swashing against the ground. She steps out besides me, and her jaw drops. Neighbors across the street have stopped just outside of their doorways to admire the same splendor of a view. A few of them look at us and at each other with amazement. It is the single most beautiful sight I've experienced in months.

There's not one snowflake in sight.

Everything outside is of its original color. The grass is a brilliant green, the streets are a smolder gray, and the roofs of the houses are actually visible. Nothing is covered by a coat of white. Nothing. I forget to breathe, my eyes watching intently. Beside me, Gammy pants hard, heaving breaths. It's a remarkable day that would have otherwise appeared normal and usual. How easily it is that you forget the things you appreciate most.

There are no dirty patches of snow waiting to melt away. There are no clear icicles hanging from the bottom of cars or from the edges of roofs. There is no frigid wind drawing your teeth to clatter. They've all vanished overnight as if they had never even been for a visit.

Overhead, in the light blue summer sky, cotton-candy clouds drift along. Birds squeal and chirp happily, wanting to be heard. The sun shines down at an angle, bouncing off each window outside. Long shadows slant from their sources, making a contrast against all else that is bright.

"It's amazing," I say.

"It's beautiful," Gammy adds in.

"How can…?"

"It's a sign of God."

And I know that it has to be. There isn't any other explanation for it. Only God could have made all that snow disappear over the course of just one night. Only Him.

Up the street, two little girls wearing summer dresses and no shoes run around, giggling, chasing each other. A dog walks along the length of the street with its tail wagging and what appears to be a smile on its face. A few of the neighbors have moved to their porch steps, sitting down, breathing in the view with their entire bodies, breathing it all in from limb to limb and skin to bone.

Our own dog Romulus joins us, but then runs out as it catches a glimpse of a squirrel. The little animal squeaks until it finds a tree to scurry up quickly. Romulus scrapes his front paws at the bark of the tree, and woofs playfully up at the squirrel.

I pick up the shovel and set it back inside, knowing that I won't need it today. I toss my winter clothes back in the crammed closet, and step back outside to continue my view.

A Volkswagon Beetle drives up and parks in front of our house. The door opens and a girl steps out. It's Jessica. She covers her eyes from the sun and then waves at me. I raise my hand with the palm facing her.

"Jeremy! Hi!"

"Hey, Jessica. What are you doing here?"

She walks up the narrow walkway that leads to our steps. Then, as she stands at the bottom, she says, "I was just stopping by to see you. Wanna go somewhere with me? It's so nice out."

"Is it cool if I go?" I ask Gammy.

"Of course."

I give her a peck on the cheek, and then walk to the car together with Jessica. Once in the car, we take off with Gammy waving at us from the porch.

"I like your grandma," she says. "She's adorable."

"Yeah, she means a lot to me. So how did you know I'd be up this early?"

"Actually, I didn't. I couldn't sleep all night, and neither could my daddy or grandma, so I figured it would be the same with you."

The way she called him her "daddy" was cute. She had stuck her tongue out between her teeth, giving me a quirky little smile. Her curvy strands of hair fall down from her head like strands of sun-lit streams. Her cheeks are bright pink and warm, full of delight in her smile. She looks beautiful, even more than ever before.

"I don't think *anyone* slept last night," I say truthfully.

"Look how beautiful it is outside!"

"It really is. I guess it's God's final gift to us before tomorrow."

She gives me another brilliant smile, full of teeth and as wide as her cheeks allow her to spread it.

"So where are you taking us?" I say.

"To feed the ducks."

A fresh loaf of bakery bread lies between us inside of a brown paper bag. I pick it up in my hands and crumple the bag back, letting the end of the bread poke out. I bring my nose to the crust and smell its surface. The warm aroma of the flour and baked dough seeps into my nostrils, making my mouth water.

"No, not *this* bread," I tell her.

"Why not?"

"This bread is too good. What are these, royal ducks?"

"I didn't know you were such a bread expert," she says with a wink and a grin.

"Oh, yes, I'm a certified bread specialist."

"Wow, I didn't think bread would tickle your fancy this much."

"Oh, I love bread! Where did you get this?"

"My grandma stayed up all night baking a few loaves. She took it out of the oven just a few hours ago. It's still warm."

"Tell her she's won my heart over."

She giggles, holding a few fingers to her nose, covering her mouth.

"You're too cute," she says, gently putting one hand on my own. Her eyes glisten, reflecting glints of sunlight.

"Can I have a piece of this?" I ask.

"Go ahead."

I tear off a chunk with my hand. The crust crackles with the twist of my fingers. The soft inner crumb stretches and then slowly pulls away. My teeth dig into the bread, making it crunch in my mouth.

"This bread is incredible," I say. "Sorry, but I don't think the ducks get to eat today."

After about a half hour of driving and half of the loaf gone, we arrive at the side of the lake. We drive parallel to its coast, with the lake to our left. Jessica takes a narrow turn towards it, sending us on a bumpy back road. Trees shade us in on each side, leaving only a trim slit of sky above our heads.

"Not many people know about this road," she says.

The car jerks from side to side, making us bump around in our seats. Then the little dirt road curves and the trees open up. A wide view of the shimmering lake appears. The water resembles a sheet of rayon fabric with thousands of sparkles spread across it randomly. Off to our left, a narrow dock-type of bridge made of wood leads to a tiny circular island. A wooden railing surrounds the bridge and all around the small islet.

"Let's go on that," I say excitedly, pointing at the artificial islet. I feel like a gleeful child, charging up energy to my face and body.

"That's the plan," she says, and we step out. The scent of nature seeps deep into my nostrils. I can smell the water, the trees, the gravel dust lifting...It all blends in like a mint to clear my sinuses. It's all so vibrant, suddenly. For once I can actually sense the sun's warmth calm my skin like a hued breath of heat.

We approach the narrow dock and hop over the small locked fence door, brown paper bag and bread still in hand. Tall plants with large leaves and small branchy trees grow from the center of the island. Yellow and red flowers are sprung from the ground, accentuating the rest of the plants. It's as if they never knew winter was here just yesterday. A circular walkway of pebbles takes us around the center. We find a metal-framed bench with a white wooded seat, and we sit down. In my mouth, I'm munching on another piece of bread.

"Give me that," she says playfully, taking the bag. "This is Ducky Island. I used to come here with my mom when I was little. We always brought bread made by my grandma and fed the ducks. Nobody else ever comes here."

A dozen or so ducks swim around on the surface of the lake, paddling their way with their feet. A few fly low over the water, quacking at the ones below. Jessica rips a small piece and throws it over the railing, into the water. Two of the quicker ducks get to it, playing tug of war with it in their beaks. The larger one wins and flutters away with it, gloating gleefully with quacks.

"Here," she says, giving me half of the bread remaining, "but this is for *them.*"

"Gotcha." I rip off a few small pieces, and throw them all at once into the water.

"I've never taken anyone else here before. It's always been just me and my mom."

"Do you still come here with her?"

"No, she died of breast cancer when I was twelve."

Saying "I'm sorry" right now would be the less caring thing to do. When my parents' died, all I heard was an apology from everyone. I didn't want that. I wanted them to ask me about them. I wanted them to care about who they were.

"How was she before she died?" I say.

"She was the perfect mom. To me at least. She never forgot to laugh. It was like a duty to her. Even when I made her mad she laughed, and actually that's when she laughed the hardest. She'd tease me about my temper and my little fits. That always put me in a better mood."

A glossy tear hangs from her bottom eyelash. It clings for a second, but then finally rolls down to the tip of her nose.

"I miss her," she says.

I know how that feels, but I don't tell her this. This is her moment. I don't want to take it away from her by reflecting on it with my own childhood memories and my yearning for my parents to be back. I let her cry while holding her with my gaze.

She sniffles softly. I bring my thumb to her face and wipe away the moisture from below one eye, and then the other. Her eyes look like glass spheres. They're trembling. She looks at me, through to me, into me, and says, "Will you hold me?"

Gently, I bring one arm around her shoulders. She tilts her head towards my chest and hugs me with both arms around my torso. In this moment I feel like I love her. I *need* to love her. I never felt like I loved a girl before, and so I know that this love is actually there. It's not something I'm fabricating at the spur of the moment just to fill an inner gap. The love I feel for her is real.

She tilts her head back a little and kisses my chin, and a tingle of static runs through it like tiny fingertips tapping. With my other hand I hold her chin in my soft palm. I kiss her on the mouth and our lips lock for a long second, unmoving. Our lips press harder before peeling away wetly.

"I love you, Jeremy," she says confidently.

I hold her tighter. "I love you, too." And those words come out spontaneously, like nature finally showing itself after all that winter.

Chapter 24

Hours later, after a full day of feeding ducks, talking, laughing and swimming in the lake in our underwear, Jessica and I drive back to my house. She walks me to my front door. Before I step in, we pause, gazing into each other's eyes silently. Hers are glossy and on the verge of tears.

"What's wrong, Jessica?"

"We won't see each other after this. Not for forty days."

"No, I guess we won't."

I hold her tiny hands in mine and bring her closer to me. Then she hugs me tightly as I move my hands, pressing them behind the small of her back.

"I had a really great time," she says.

"Me too. I had the most fun swimming."

She gives out a tiny laugh. Her cheeks turn rosy and she smiles up at me with her chin pressed against my chest.

"Yeah, me too," she admits.

I kiss her forehead. Then I kiss between her brows. Then down to the tip of her nose. Finally my lips find hers. My eyes are closed as I'm kissing her, but I can feel her lips widen with a smile without having to see them. I lift her higher so that her face is above my own, and she hugs tighter, wrapping her arms around my shoulders. More tears drip from her eyes and fall down to my cheeks.

I put her down and I ask, "What's wrong?"

She sniffles, her face pouts sadly, and her eyes widen. "This is going to be so hard. I'm scared, Jeremy," she says, crying.

"I know, Jessica. I am too, but we'll get through this. Just keep praying, and keep strong. You can do this. I know you can. Don't cry. Smile for me."

"I can't smile. It's just too hard."

"Hey, what's the hardest part about eating a vegetable?"

"Hu?" she says, trying to digest the random question.

"The wheelchair."

She bursts into a surprised laugher, her face frowning and smiling, both at the same time. I'm glad that we can at least share the same sense of humor.

"See, I knew you could smile," I say. I stretch my face down towards hers and kiss the tears off of her cheeks.

The door opens behind us. It creaks noisily, and then clicks shut.

"There you are. I was beginning to worry about you," Gammy says from behind.

"Oh, I just lost track of time. Sorry."

"That's all right. A boy's gotta have his fun. What did you guys do today?" she asks.

"We fed the ducks up at Crystal Clear Lake."

"For twelve hours?"

I look at my watch and see that it's almost seven at night.

"And we improvised a few activities," Jessica adds in.

Dusk is falling upon the sky, turning everything to a reddish tan color. The sun is slowly fading away into the right, falling behind buildings and houses. There's something odd about this image, and it takes me a second to realize what.

"Gammy," I say, "doesn't the sun fall into the west?"

"Yes, why?"

"Isn't that direction east?" I say, pointing with a finger at the mellow rays of diminishing sunlight.

She thinks for a moment, trying to remember. Her mouth opens a little as if to answer, but then hesitates. "It is," she finally says, mesmerized. "Oh my dear God, it is."

The skin on my back turns into prickly goosebumps and the hairs on my arms stand on ends.

Gammy turns to Jessica, saying, "I think you better go home before it gets dark. And hurry. The sun's falling fast."

"Okay," she says, stepping back. She seems afraid and maybe even confused. "Good night, Jeremy. Good night, Mrs. Christ."

"Good night, dear," Gammy says, pressing her lips with a pained smile.

"Jessie, hold on," I say, still holding on to her hand. I pull her back towards me and hug her tightly, taking in every scent of hers. Her smell. Her touch. Her presence. I try to conserve them all for those few seconds so that they will last me forever. "*Now* I can say good night." In that, we were saying our last good-byes.

She leaves.

Gammy and I step in and she looks up at me. Her lined face is delicate but worried. Her skin is stressed in a way that reveals that to me.

"We better lock all the doors and windows. I hope Jessica makes it home in time."

DESPERATION

Chapter 25

I am in this large, empty parking lot where the ground is made of dark gray asphalt that expands to swallow infinity. The white-painted stripes on the ground are faded, making it hard to define each parking spot. The lighting is dim, and the sky is coated by foggy clouds. In front of me is a large theater with dull lights that flicker on and off. The sign on the front tilts crookedly, about to fall off its hinges. The sign reads Circus Theatre.

After two steps, I am already inside, transported in an instant. The interior is dilapidated and worn out. The once colorful wallpaper with randomly dotted flowers is stripped here and there randomly, leaving crumbly patches of the wall showing beneath.

A circular ticket booth with a glass window on the front faces me, empty. The entire place is lifeless, not a person around. I walk on the sanguine colored carpet in search of the bathroom. My bladder squeezes down on itself in needle-prick bites.

I find a crusty white door and push it. The door stops, hitting hard against something, and swings back my direction. I move aside, avoiding its path. A tall, dark-skinned man stands at the doorway, blocking the entrance to the bathroom. The tip of the man's head brushes the top of the doorframe. He looks down at me with marble-white eyes as sharp as kitchen knives. The man's upper lip is thin, nearly missing, while his lower one pooches. His cheekbones bulge, and his face has a glossy olive oil coat to it.

I step back, gasping. The man advances silently and disappears somewhere behind me.

Inside the bathroom, both the floor tiles and the ones covering the walls are cracked. A tile from the wall slips and falls to the ground, breaking into several scattering pieces. The urinals on the walls are piss-stained, and their handles spotted with rust.

Facing me, at the very end of the bathroom are two stalls made of wooden planks and metal frames. I step in the one to the right, and the door hinges squeak. I close the door but there is no lock.

Instead of a toilet, inside is a square-shaped bucket hanging from a garden faucet that sticks out of the wall. The ground is coated by several dried puddles of urine along with a few streaks of chocolate brown stains.

The bucket is already half filled with bowel wastes and foul stricken fluids. Dark clumps of solid turds bob up and down in the feces-infested liquid. I piss in the bucket, and my urine makes a deep pouring sound as it dives into the muddy contents. The level of the brown fluid rises, inching its way to the rim of the bucket slowly. Then the bucket begins to sway back and forth with the contents sloshing inside of it. It starts off gently at first, but as I continue to urinate, the swings of the bucket get wider and wider. A big wave of watery shit splashes out, and the level of the soupy feces continues to crawl towards the top.

The chunky soup starts to overflow like a bathtub with the faucet left on for too long. The liquid cascades over the edges and splashes to the ground. The bucket rushes for another swing, moments away from toppling over and spilling everything to the ground. Before it can, I grab it by the corners with my thumbs dipping into the disgusting liquids. I set it down gently and shake off my hands, sprinkling the brown urine off my fingers.

I pull on the roll of toilet paper and rip off a length of it. I step out wiping my hands, and notice that the stalls are no longer facing the same direction they were before. They're now set along a different side of the wall. Also, the bathroom isn't long and rectangular anymore. It has widened and squared off.

In front of the bathroom sinks, I see a very large man sitting at a square table with sleek iron legs.

"Take a seat. Please," the fat man says, gesturing to the iron chair facing him. His voice sounds as if his mouth were full of curdling saliva. As he breathes, solid globs of mucus gurgle in his nose forming a raspy, wheezing husk. I sit down, resting my palms on the table.

The man's face is sweaty, and his oily skin has a reddish tint to it. He has short black hair that clings to his scalp from its dampness. His lips are rouge, a color that resembles flames. His chin is round, and below it, a roll of fat drapes, forming a very tender double chin. The man wears a greasy undershirt with oily stains smudged all over. Over the undershirt a short-sleeved, unbuttoned shirt covers the man's shoulders, changing colors and designs with each glimpse I take, all opaque and lifeless.

A large chessboard sits at the center of the table. A square board on top of a square table in the middle of a square bathroom. Only the man is round.

"Care to play?" the round man asks with a wide grin, his teeth as dull as rusted spoons.

I don't answer. I just sit there motionless, facing him.

"You can be white," he says, still urging on the game. From beside him he pulls out a brown leather medicine bag. It's the type of bag you would picture doctors carrying around years and years ago, at a time when it was still possible to die from the flu.

With his swollen-sausage fingers he pulls out a statuette shaped like an angel carrying a sword. He begins to set up the board, tapping the base of each piece on its appropriate square.

After my sixteen pieces are set up, he starts to array his black pieces in two rows. Only they're not painted black. They are actually a reddish brown color. His pieces are in the shape of tiny imps and demonic creatures. It is then that I realize that I'm facing the devil in a game of chess.

I run out of the bathroom with a scream struggling to find a voice in my throat. The door swats open and I find myself outside, circled by a blinding white light.

I wake up in my dark room, realizing it was just a dream, but only the beginning of the real nightmare.

Chapter 26

Three lines of strange words dash across the message board in the kitchen in bold white chalk. The scratchy letters are sprawled to cover most of the area on the little blackboard. They read: MAKE A DEATH WISH AND HEAR THE SOUND OF DESPERATION.

A sheet of chills rolls up my back, bringing me to a cold, hard shiver. This isn't just a joke. Not a funny one at least. The only two people in the house are Gammy and me, and I don't think this is the type of gag Gammy would scribble for me to read. No, it's not a joke at all.

But then who wrote it?

My saliva thickens, slicking up my palate and coating my tongue, and I feel the entire room wave in and out around me. It stretches and expands, and then waves back in as if the walls were made of rubber.

Far behind me I hear Gammy's slippers shuffle on the floor. Spontaneously, I grab the chalk eraser and wipe away the words, disintegrating them to streaks of fine dust. I take the stick of chalk with my fingers and write "40 DAYS" at the top of the board. Below the writing, off to the left, I scratch a little white line to indicate the first day of Judgment.

"What are you writing there?" Gammy asks from behind.

"I'm keeping track of the days. Only thirty-nine left," I say with a dry tone. Not a speck of humor on my lips.

"Oh I see. I don't know how much that will help, though."

"What do you mean?"

"Well..." she hesitates. "Forty is an abstract number. Usually, when the age of a person or a certain number is unknown, it gets replaced by the number forty."

"Like Ali Baba and the forty thieves?"

"Exactly. It's very likely that there weren't forty thieves at all."

"So what does this mean to us?"

"Maybe nothing. Maybe this period will last exactly for forty days as predicted, but not necessarily. It could go on for less."

"Or longer," I say, terrified by the thought. Just waking up with the dream I had last night makes me want to send everything to hell and give up. That dream alone put enough fear in me to last forty days and beyond.

"Are you hungry?" Gammy says.

"No. Not at all." I hadn't eaten anything yesterday except for bread, but I couldn't stomach any food right now. Maybe not for a while. I feel hollow inside my stomach, but it also feels impenetrable and on guard. If I ate any food I probably wouldn't be able to digest it.

"Me either. I guess we both have a loss of appetite."

Just that instant, a loud thump bangs at the door. We both turn to it and stare. I step towards it, but Gammy puts a hand to my arm.

"Don't go outside."

"What was that?"

"I don't know, but it's better if we don't find out."

"Do you hear that?"

A low murmur rises and glides to sting my ears. A small vibration—as resilient as a hum—resonates next to my ears. It's a low pitch, droning as softly as a hushed, raspy buzz. I can't tell whether it's coming from outside or if it's inside my head. Then I hear a long, desperate moan grumble painfully. It's more than just one voice. The groans waver, as if trying to create a chorus of disturbing howls. The voices sing a restless tone, and then more and more voices gather, adding to the contorted and pained sound.

"It's coming from outside," Gammy says, as if reassuring herself.

I step back and grab Gammy's hand. Mine is trembling, but Gammy's keeps sturdy and strong. Feeling her strength eases me. Little by little the moans subside. As the devilish choir becomes softer and softer, it begins to chant together a vibration that seems to hang at the throat. The chanted sound wavers, and then it becomes "hush...hush...hush..." The chants lull softer and softer, leaving a ringing in my ears.

Silence. Uncomfortable and stiff.

Then suddenly the windows begin to rattle and the doors rumble with continuous banging and knocking. The noise becomes a thunderstorm, surging through the walls and rattling my nerves with its vibrations. The windows shake like trembling sheets of water. Outside the windows, darkness has taken total control. The sun has been blown out like a candle. I look at my watch, reading that it's just a few minutes past noon. Unless, that is, it's midnight.

Then the noises begin to unify. Slowly, the pounding takes up a rhythm. The house is bombarded by hits and poundings of a steady beat. The beat starts off in a rhythmical, unhurried flow, like the heartbeat of a man dying a slow and painless death. But then, little by little it begins to pick up speed with each hit. My hand squeezes harder on Gammy's, crushing it inside my palm. I can't help it. The drumming becomes faster and faster, soon enough matching my own heart rate.

Then, even faster.

It sounds like a stadium filled with tens of thousands of people, all stomping their feet on the ground. My heart feels like it's going to explode, and the house feels like it's going to crumble to pieces along with it like a sort of devious agreement. *I will if you will*, my heart seems to say to the house. I just hope that neither of them happens. I can't even imagine what it would be if whatever was outside broke through the walls and got in

Then, when my body can't take it any longer, I shout at the top of my lungs.

My voice can't compete with the drilling thunder that overpowers it, but I shout anyways. I try to scream louder to match the noises, but I can't. I can't even hear my own voice. I just want the drumming to end. By now Gammy's hand has slipped out of my grip, unable to sustain the pain of mine crushing it. My fists tighten and my knuckles bulge, still with my voice screaming. The thunder of noises is unwilling to give in.

Romulus comes out of Gammy's room and starts barking. It's a nasty, inaudible roar that tells me he's willing to tear whatever's outside, flesh from bone. Just his enraged, snarling face tells me what his barks would sound like if only they could be heard. His lips ripple back in a snarl, showing his fangs smothered in saliva. The hair around his neck stands straight, arcing down his back. Finally he howls as if to define his territory.

Gammy covers her ears with her little hands. She seems to be screaming too with her mouth open, but it's impossible to tell for sure. She shakes her head back and forth. The white curls of her hair joggle on top of her head.

My voice is starting to run out, and my lungs begin to burn.

"Make a death wish," the message had said. I didn't intend for my screaming to be that wish, but now it feels as if this is how I'm going to die: with my lungs burnt to red rashes, my heart exploded, and the eardrums in my head burst. I can't take it any longer. The constant ramming at the walls has become impossible to disobey. It instigates a quarrel, and that's exactly what I'm giving it.

Gammy runs to her room, still plugging her ears as tightly as possible.

My throat feels like I've been swallowing sand. A gritty sensation scratches at it from the inside.

Seconds later, Gammy runs back out with a leather-covered book in her arms. Amidst all this chaos, it takes me a moment to realize it's a Bible. She smacks it down on the counter and the pages just fan apart by themselves. Gammy puts a flat finger down on the page given to her and begins to read. Her voice roars above all else, and somehow I can hear her words perfectly.

"But the Lord is in his holy temple; let all the earth be silent before him" (Habakkuk 2:20).

Silence.

The windows suddenly become still, the doors stop trembling, Romulus's howling ceases, and even I finish screaming. My scream had run out of breath just as Gammy had finished speaking her words. Everything cut off in an instant, and all it took was a phrase. A quote. A scripture.

"A prayer," Gammy says out of breath and her voice quivering, "is all it takes to get through this."

I pant hard. My eyes are watery and my lips are dry and flaky.

"How did you open it up to the right page so fast?"

"I didn't have to. It opened itself up to me."

My breathing is heavy, as if I just finished springing a quarter mile. I approach Gammy and hold her in my arms.

"Thank you," I say. "I couldn't take it any longer."

"Neither could I, Jeremy. Neither could I."

I let go of Gammy and step to the window to peer out into the blackness. It's hard to make much of anything out. All the shapes seem to be blurring into one black wash engulfing everything. The wind howls outside, whistling a deathly tune. It's a chilling sound. Far off into the distances, blurry shapes that take form of human shadows run around in scattered directions.

"There's people outside," I say to Gammy. She moves to the window and sets her hands on my shoulders.

"They're not people. A person couldn't survive out there. This is the only safe place. Inside a house, surrounded by the spirit of God."

"Why isn't God out there then?"

"He's letting *them* run the outside world for now. You have to remember: this is a test."

A test. The sound of the word makes my stomach churn and my mind nauseous. So far, this has already been the hardest test I've ever had to face.

"So those are…" I say, unable to finish my own sentence.

"Demons, yes."

"I'm going to call Jessica. She must be terrified by now. She needs me."

I pick the receiver in my hand, and cradle it to my ear. What I hear is not a dial tone. Instead I hear a chuckling laugher wheezing its breath into curls of grunts. It's a disgusting laugh that sounds sickly ill. A woman's voice then screams, followed by more inhumane grunting. The woman's voice begins to cry and beg. She's shrieking for help, screaming names incoherently. The laugher turns maniacal. I can't listen to it anymore. I slam the receiver back down, and push it away with what feels like my muscles twitching.

"The phones are down," I tell Gammy with my lungs expanding and contracting heavily.

"I'm not surprised. The only things that seem to be running are the electricity and water. The different utility companies set up their resources to make sure we have all of that for the next forty days. And if those happen to fail us, we're prepared. We have plenty of candles, jugs of water and even that camping gas stove."

I wouldn't want to resort to using any of those things, but hearing her mention them makes me feel more secure. Going back to the window, I look up at the infinite black sky.

Far, far away the moon floats in its solitude. It's a silver circle, alone in the blackened sky. I look everywhere else, but see no stars around it. How very cruel the world turns when the sun comes down and there are no stars in the sky. That moon. Tonight she's no friend of ours, as she never was.

Chapter 27

According to the blackboard, we're now on the fourth day of what feels like hell. It's hard to keep track of the days because outside the window it's always dark. Since the sun doesn't rise or set, I have to go by the clock, and sometimes I can't remember if only twelve hours went by or a whole day. Gammy was right. Forty days may not be forty at all once all this is over.

To pass the time I usually read a book or play board games or cards with Gammy. Under normal circumstances I would be reading a Stephen King novel or something else along the line of horror, but it's impossible for me to read such a book without being overwhelmed by a fear that goes beyond the pages. It's too easy for me to be terrified by the simplest phrase of such a book.

My games with Gammy are often interrupted by the noises that have by now become a routine. At night I would awaken to the sound of something tapping at my window. I would pretend to be asleep and the tapping eventually would end after a few minutes, but never without a sinister snicker following it.

Even in my sleep I can't flee the horror. I've been having terrible nightmares ever since the one about the game of chess in the bathroom. I had a dream where three imps were squatting over my carcass, picking at my meat for food. It's a constant, twenty-four hour incubus. There is no escape from it. Praying is the only thing that helps me get my mind at ease. I pray as much as possible. Most of the time, I recite Our Father. I read from the Bible every day and close with a rosary, but still the nightmare persists.

Gammy and I are playing cards in the living room. The room is quiet, filled only by our glum breathing and the occasional, uncomfortable smile on our faces. Then, from behind me I hear a thumping sound. We stop playing for a second, and as I set the cards down on the coffee table, Gammy's hand reaches for her Bible, ready to dismiss whatever rumble should arise.

There is silence for a few seconds, but then the noise repeats itself. It's a low thud against the wall that comes through hollow. Then the sound takes up a slow rhythm.

Thump. Thump. Thump.

After the third hit on the wall, I finally decide to turn around. I twist my neck, peering over my right shoulder. There, where the noise is coming from, Romulus stands limply on all fours. His legs are sprawled widely like a table with loose joints. I turn my torso to get a better look, and I notice that it's him making the thudding sounds. He is swinging his neck back and forth, banging his head against the wall.

Thump, thump, thump.

I stand up and head towards him. His head bobs a bit harder at every hit, a bit faster every time. His whole body sways out and then droops back towards the wall, each time smacking his head with enough impact to have it bounce off.

Wearily, I step closer towards him. His head stops bobbing. As I step just a few feet closer, his legs close in and he makes little awkward steps, turning his body around to face me. His posture is drooped as if he were sick or dehydrated. His eyes roll back in their sockets, leaving only two blank marbles in their place.

"Romulus? What's wrong?"

"What's the matter with Romulus?" Gammy asks from far behind me.

"I don't know. He looks sick. Real sick."

I extend my hand trying to reach for his face, intending to pet him. As my hand gets closer, his lips twitch and his eyes roll back to show his pupils. His retinas are no longer the beautiful clear blue color they once were. They're gray, fogged into a horrible depth.

His lips curl back displaying a menacing snag of teeth. They're yellowish and sharp, but he's not growling through them yet. His eyes don't seem to be looking at me. They appear lost in their fogginess.

I take another step and that's when Romulus' jaw snaps open and shut, giving off an angry yelp of saliva. His lips smack, and as he withdraws them to a full stretch, a thin sheet of saliva rolls back with their peeling. His nose twitches and then snuffs out. A bit of bloody mucus shoots out of his nostril and lands on the ground.

The fog dissipates from his eyes, but his irises are still the same color gray of old asphalt. His pupils widen and become sharp. Romulus' thick, white coat springs up on his back like thousands of steady needles. He takes a step towards me, and his claws tap on the ground. His posture suddenly becomes stiff, no longer drooping as if he were to keel over.

"Romulus…" I say. My voice is trembling.

From behind me, Gammy gives off a tiny cry upon seeing our dog's new appearance. Romulus' face snaps in her direction and an evil, snarly smile forms on his lips. Only it's not exactly a smile. A smile conveys joy, and the shape of his lips forms only a distraught hate. His legs twitch, and an instant later he bolts towards her faster than my eyes can follow his movements.

Gammy freezes as the monstrous Alaskan wolf rushes towards her. His legs buckle and then retract like springs. They extend, shooting him through the air. He's too fast for me to be able to tackle him before he can leap on Gammy. Instead, without even giving it a thought, my hand reaches for a foldable metal stool beside me. I grab it by its back handle, and launch it, aiming for Romulus.

The stool hurls through the air, whacking Romulus across the face split seconds before digging his canines into Gammy's neck. Romulus yelps and he is jerked sideways by the hit, falling to the ground. He lands on his feet with intense agility, and his paws slide on the wooden floor for a moment. Then he gains grip on the ground with the bottom of his roughed paws, and he finally stops sliding. He gives me a crooked look and snarls.

His lips are wet and glossy with gluey saliva. He looks at me, then at Gammy, and then at me again. Instantly, his legs kick in and he charges at me. The shape of his body lurches like a racehorse giving it all it's got to finish the race. He stretches and compresses his body with each leap, but then he jumps, lurching through the air towards me.

His weight impacts against my upper torso, pushing me back against the counter. My back hits the cornered edge of it, shooting a knotted rope of pain up my backbone. My left elbow swipes backwards, striking a pile of dishes. The pile wobbles and a few crash to the floor.

Romulus has me pinned against the counter, and I can't do anything but try to keep him off. His face is inches away from my own with a mouth wide enough to swallow my arm. His legs scramble against the floor while I try to push him off with a hand to his chest. My other hand has grappled him by the neck, fiercely fighting him off of me. Curls of saliva splatter out as he snaps his jaw open and shut.

I know that if he bites me even once, it's all going to be over for me.

The entire structure of his face has diverged into what resembles a wild animal. He is no longer the domesticated housedog he once was. He's become the wolf that his instincts tell him to be. Struggling with every intention to gnaw at my face, his neck shakes and pushes forward. His snout chomps out, each time getting closer and closer to my nose.

My fingers slip from his neck and his face lunges forward with his jaws spread, ready to shut again and tear a chunk of flesh off my cheek. I tilt my neck just in time, missing his bite. I curl my weight around him, grappling his chest from behind with my arms. He tries to shake me off and his neck jerks more, going from shoulder to shoulder. Luckily, my arms are just out of his bite's reach. He tries to twist his neck to bite my fingers but can't reach them. I tumble to the ground, bringing him down with me. We wrestle and we roll around, each taking turns on being on top.

I still have him gripped tightly by his torso and he continually tries to get me off. Beside me I see the plates that have fallen from the counter. Some are cracked in half or in several pieces, but one is still mainly intact with only a small piece chipped off the edge of it. I stretch one arm out to grab for it, and I swat it against Romulus' head. The plate hitting him makes a flat *clunk* sound but it doesn't break.

Romulus is jolted by the hit and his front legs twitch. I slide on the ground, my clothes tugging and tearing as I try to clamp him down. I push my weight on top of him with my chest. One of his front legs is clamped under his body along with my arm.

While all of this is happening, I catch a glimpse of Gammy, terrified and screaming. I stretch my hand holding the plate all the way back, and then I bring it down one more time against Romulus' temple. Clunk. Romulus's face twitches. The plate doesn't break, so I bring it back down on him harder. Clunk! A large chunk cracks off in a V-shape. When I bring it up for another hit, I realize that I'm now holding a plate cracked in two unequal halves.

Romulus' back retracts and then pushes out fiercely, all the while kicking me with his hind legs. That manages to push me off him, and I roll onto my back. He struggles to get to his feet and then lurches on top of me, still snarling a hideous double row of teeth. I clutch onto his collar with both hands. I squeeze hard and push out, making him gag. Romulus coughs a sickly choke of air. He looks down on me and I can see little red veins branch out to surround his pupils.

His upper lip pulls back in the front like curtains unveiling two hideous fangs. Despite my knuckles pressing on his throat, he pushes forward with his neck. The two rows of teeth grit on one another, and a low, droning roar escapes from between. A tingly ache surrounds my arms and muscles. I feel my muscles weakening and trembling. I can't hold him off any longer. He pushes even harder as if going forth against a water current, and now I can taste his spoiled salmon breath on my lips. Rapidly, his teeth clatter in compulsive little twitches. His teeth graze my face, and my skin feels strung and tight.

His cold, wet nose snuffs at my cheek, right below my left eye. His sharp, tiny whiskers on his muzzle form pin pricks into my face. I give out a scream of suffocated pain. I feel like crying out but I am too enveloped by terror. My mouth bursts out with a shuffle of indescribable sounds. I give off a painful shriek joined by a lamented cry.

"Please...Gammy, help! Help me!"

Whack.

The end of the stool I had thrown at Romulus earlier slams against his cheek. It's not a very hard whack, but it's enough to jolt Romulus. I push him off of me and I see Gammy standing above me. She retreats her arms, holding the chair high over her head. Then she slams the metal stool down fiercely, bashing against Romulus' temple. Romulus' body convulses and his legs kick, springing out and back again.

Then he becomes still.

I get up slowly, struggling over my own weakness. I put my hand on top of the counter for leverage, but my hand lands over the handle of a large kitchen knife instead. My grip slips off the counter and I fall back down to the ground.

Just as I hit the floor, Romulus jerks up and jumps back at me. My hands clutch the handle of the knife again, pointing it out in front of me. The blade burrows into his stomach. He gives out a slobbery wheezing noise. He puts forth a last effort of struggle, but he manages no more than a yelp, splattering blood from his lips.

Romulus' blood is black like petroleum with only the slightest tint of red to it. I pull out the blade, meaning to stab him again, but his stiff body just flops over without life. The black blood drizzles out of the cut, boiling as it laps to the ground. Little bubbles emerge from it, popping as they reach the surface. Seconds later the liquid dries up, staining the off-beat brown tiles permanently.

"What should we do with him?" I say to Gammy. My face feels flushed hot and prickly with sweat. There is a tremble to my voice, I can feel it. It's a tremble that speaks out for the cruel loss of a companion.

"I...I don't know."

"We need to bury him outside. I'm going to do it."

"No, Jeremy. We *can't*."

"I don't care what's out there! I have to bury him. Those bastards out there fucked with his mind, and now he's dead in our house. We can't leave him in here."

My urge for wanting to bury him is more out of respect for Romulus than for not wanting a dead animal in the house. I look through the storage closet, crammed with any "just in case" material, and I grab an old shovel with dirt clumps still clinging to its edges.

"You'll be dead before you can even hit the ground with it if you go out there," she says tonelessly, "and worse yet, you'll be disobeying God." Her voice stops me before I can reach the door.

"Then what are we going to do with him?"

"I don't know, but he's starting to smell already. We have to get rid of him. That smell is too foul."

The fumes of Romulus' stench had already penetrated my nose when I first stabbed him. It's mostly the blood that gave a sickly, liver-breath smell. Already, around Romulus' wound, the flesh is begging to rot, and the stench thickens, jamming itself in my throat. Gammy is right, we need to get rid of him.

"Then what? Throw him outside the window so that *they* can feed on him? I couldn't let that happen to him."

"No. I wouldn't want to do that either. Besides, if we opened a door or a window, even for just a second, I'm afraid they'll get in. We can't risk that."

Gammy gives the fireplace a look. She is unsure, and I know what she is going to propose.

"We'll have to burn him."

Unfortunately, I can't argue with that. Already I'm covering my mouth and nose with one hand.

Romulus' whole body couldn't fit in the fireplace all at once, though. The fireplace is small, big enough to fit just a couple of logs, and Romulus is almost half my size. I grab a handsaw from a toolbox, knowing—unforgivably—what the only thing that can be done is. I look at the saw in dismay for a second, studying the spots of rust that dot over its blade. Solemnly, I fall to my knees next to Romulus. Gammy grabs a large towel, and I lift Romulus' fleshy body so that she can slide it beneath. It feels like lifting a big lump of dough.

The saw's scaly teeth dig into Romulus's flesh, ripping it apart with the first cut of the blade. It takes only a few minutes to cut him in two, all the while gagging and covering my nose with my shirt. At one point the combination of the stench and having to watch the blood gush out and the intestines flop and snap produces a lurching, empty bubble in my stomach. But I don't throw up. I hold it back knowing that it would make things so much harder if I did, even if it got rid of the nausea.

We burn his lower half first, using almost half a tin of lighter fluid. With the touch of a lit match, his body flames up in big plumes. A thick cloud of smoke climbs up the chimney, and the smell overrides the room. The stench resembles that of a burning dumpster filled with garbage and large amounts of rotten meat. It takes only a few minutes for the lower part of Romulus' body to incinerate and then disappear.

"Why don't they come in through the chimney?" I say to Gammy, a bit perplexed by the thought. "I mean whatever's outside. Couldn't they climb down it?"

"I'm not sure, but I think it's because there's a white cross painted on the chimney top."

"Really? I never noticed it before. When was it painted?"

"Oh, a long time ago. Your father did it when you were still young."

I grab Romulus' upper torso and toss it on top of the ashes. This time I don't use any lighter fluid, I just throw in a lit match. His flesh blazes on all the same, and Romulus' hateful expression burns from his face as the flames lick it away.

150

Chapter 28

I sit on my bed in my room with my shoulders slouched over in front of me. I feel worn out. Both my body and mind ache painfully. I feel so physically and mentally torn apart that I don't think I can go on any longer. According to the message board we're in the seventh day, and I don't even know if I can believe that. It feels like it's been months, not days, that have passed.

This is what Hell must feel like. Hell must be a place where you're filled with constant suffering and you don't know how long it's been since you first came in. And the darkness. Hell must be the darkest of all places. How could it not be? The darkness is so terribly inviting to these fears, these cringes, these terrors that constantly return. I can't even be alone in this room without feeling a cold breath creeping down the nape of my neck. There is at least one difference between this and Hell, though. That difference is prayer: The ability to talk to God and ask him for strength. I don't think you can pray in Hell. It wouldn't be Hell if you could. Prayer is the request for salvation, and there is no such thing in the fiery pits of damnation.

As I lean back on my bed, I can feel a slight wobble underneath me. I step off and crouch low to the ground to examine the legs of my bed. I remember placing the Bible Gammy bought me last Christmas under one of them. I raise the bed's weight of the book, slide the Bible out from beneath, and let the bed clunk down at a crooked tilt.

The book is no bigger than my palm and about twice as thick as my hand. It was the perfect width to support the tilt. I don't even remember how that leg turned out to be so much shorter than the rest. I think we bought the bed cheap from a garage sale just two years earlier, and that's how it came. For all that while I actually slept with the tilt, until finally

Gammy gave me the Bible and I promised to her that I'd use it. It was a perfect fit, so I just slid it under and the problem was fixed.

I take another book from my shelf, and I place it under the broken leg. The book is a little too thin though, and the bed still holds a slight bob.

Now, as I observe the front cover of the Bible, I see a deep crease pressed into it, a small squared indentation at the center of it. I wipe off the dust from the cover and binding. The pages are still crisp and cling to one another, making it hard to peel each apart. I open it to the first page of scripture, skipping the intro. I realize that this is the first time I've ever opened a Bible on my own.

"Genesis," it says. "1: The origin of the world and of the Human Race."

Before I go on, I walk to my desk drawer. Along with the Bible, Gammy had also bought me a gold chain with a small golden cross. I wore the chain almost every day, taking it off when getting in the shower or when heading to bed, except I've never put on the cross before. Now I have a strong urge to do so. I set the book aside, and slip the end of the chain through the hook of the charm and clasp the chain around my neck, letting the golden crucifix hang from it. I admire it for a second, pressed between my fingers, and I like the way it shimmers. I pick up my Bible, and I turn towards the bed-

I gasp, freezing still. In less then a split second a wave of shivers rolls through my skin. My hold on the small Bible loosens and it falls from my grasp. It hits the ground with a silent thud, muffled. I pant hard and my eyes turn watery, fixed on the window above the head of my bed.

My breath comes out in silent whimpers that resemble the quick breathing of a small child moments before he's about to cry. I can do no more than stare with eyes wide and breathe my uncomfortable breath. I try to move but I can't. My mouth is parted, lips and jaw quivering.

From the window, two reflecting yellow eyes stare back into mine. These eyes, hovering in the center of my window, seem to be glowing. Their shine is dull, but it seeps through the thick glass like torches in the darkness. Below them, a wide mouth full of teeth widens to form a self-satisfied smirk. The teeth are sharp, each filed to a point that could penetrate steel. There is a slim gap between the upper file of teeth and the bottom, and strings of saliva connect the two rows.

The diabolical smile widens, revealing the slightest bit of its greenish-gray gums. The face's pointy nose presses against the glass of the window. Its mouth breathes heavy puffs of air that fog up the glass and then fade away. The lips spread even wider, and a slobbery wet tongue curls and twists inside the creature's mouth. It comes out and licks the upper row of its teeth. The tongue glides across them, leaving behind a snail-trail of saliva.

The demon's hands come up fast and swat flat on the glass, their palms facing me. I gasp and jump back at the slam of his hands. The knuckles bulge much wider than the fingers themselves, which are deformed and crooked.

I feel like screaming, but all I can manage is my own whimpering. I crouch down to reach for the Bible, but my face never leaves the creature's own. The demon is motionless except for his large pupils that roll around in their sockets, following my slow, careful movements.

As I'm crouching down, my hand feeling around to find the Bible, the demon snarls a terrible grimace. He—it—that thing appears so terribly menacing, like a starved beast ready to eat even its own kind. My eyes are fixed at its wildness, submerged in a puddle of tears. I gulp back, except there is no saliva in my mouth to be swallowed.

I stand up slowly, still looking at those glowing eyes. My bones cringe and my joints pop. The demon's lips widen to form two sharp corners of a large, looming grin. The imp hisses out a wheezy breath of air that resembles the laugh of someone who has smoked a thousand too many cigarettes in his life.

Looking at his glowing eyes jolts me into a flashback that lasts the length-span of a flash. I remember having seen this same demon before. Not just one *like* it, but the same exact one. It was following me the night I was walking to Ben's, and now it's come back to mock me.

I step forward, approaching the bed. I plant my knees on the mattress, and as I pace forward, pressing grooves into the sheets, fear trembled only harder within me. The demon's eyes focus on me, never blinking. Never leaving my presence. Never assuming anything but a mocking glare.

The creature's wheezy laugher returns, but this time it's less of a hiss and more of a cackle. The breathiness from it dissipates, and now his laughter clucks at me in a sardonic tone as if to say, *What are you going to do about it, Jeremy? What could you possibly do? You're in there, and I'm out here. If you break through the window I will devour you and pluck the meat from my teeth with your bones.*

The laughter increases in volume. The shimmering eyes persist with their glow. Inside his mouth I can see the snail-like tongue flicker and curl around. The demon begins swatting at the window with his palms. With each slap, the mock in his laughter grows, expanding like a dry sponge soaking in blood.

I cringe all over, not at the loud smacking of his hands, but at the sound of the disgusting laughs. I reach closer to the window, bringing my face inches away from the glass. The sight of his blazing eyes seeps through to reach me. My lips remain closed, my teeth clasped shut, making my cheekbones bulge.

My hand reaches for the string beside the window. I yank on it, and a wall of plastic shades shoots down between me and that horrible face. The vision of him is gone, but now the laughter becomes even more persistent and derisive, knowing that it succeeded in scaring me off. My knuckles tighten around the Bible, and instantly I open it, not knowing what page I am looking for, but sure that it will be the right one.

I slam the small book on the windowsill and the pages shuffle open. Immediately, I know what to read. The words jump out at me with designation. My lips move and I begin to mouth the scripture: "Finally, be strong in the Lord and in his mighty power. Put on the full armor of God so that you can take your stand against the devil's schemes. For our struggle is not against flesh and blood, but against the rulers, against the authorities, against the powers of his dark world and against the spiritual forces of evil in the heavenly realms."

At first my voice comes through cracked and shaken. It is of a weak caliber, but the strong words that I speak send out a powerful shrill to the demon. The voice outside stops laughing, and instead takes up a shriek, discomforting and painful to the ears. I keep reading, gaining more confidence with each word.

"Therefore put on the full armor of God, so that when the day of evil comes, you may be able to stand your ground, and after you have done everything, to stand. Stand firm then, with the belt of truth buckled around your waist, with the breastplate of righteousness in place, and with your feet filled with the readiness that comes from the gospel of peace. In addition to all this, take up the shield of faith, with which you can extinguish all the flaming arrows of the evil one. Take the helmet of salvation and the sword of Spirit, which is the word of God. And pray in the Spirit on all occasions with all kinds of prayers and requests. With this in mind, be alert and always keep on praying for all the saints" (Ephesians 6:10-18).

By the end of the last sentence, the shrieking has faded away into the abyss of darkness. My body is rigid, strong, and full of spirit. My legs are firm and steady. The demon hasn't won after all. I have come ahead in this battle, and with this victory I've gathered enough courage to finish this war.

Chapter 29

I've finally given up on dashing the number of days on the black board in the kitchen. I don't see what the point of it is anymore since I can't even trust the number of white lines. I woke up early today around seven and went straight to the kitchen. When I looked at the board, I knew something wasn't right. Just yesterday I remember slashing the twelfth mark in a row. This morning there were only eight. It's impossible to keep track of the days this way.

Right now I'm in the bathroom. I step out of the shower, left surrounded by a fine mist of steam. The entire mirror is fogged up, and anything reflecting off of it appears silvery gray. With my hand I swIpe away a streak of steam.

What I see draws me aback, and my chest seems to implode with a breath. I look again, and the reflection turns back to normal. It's just me looking at me. At first glance, my reflection's eyes seemed to be blazing with greed, his jaw structure more defined, and his upper lip was so thin that it was almost invisible. That was the face of the man who killed my father. The same exact face. But it's gone now, replaced by my own.

I wipe more of the dew away from the mirror and lean closer to it, bringing my nose inches from the glass. I stare into my deep brown eyes. It's a stare that goes on infinitely, seeping through the darkness of my own pupils. What's in there? What is in those eyes? I stare at my reflection, making sure that it really is me in there.

I pull away, distancing myself from my other self. I step to face the toilet bowl, and from the corner of my eye I catch a glimpse of the mirror. I realize then that my mind is playing tricks on me. Out of the corner of my eye, my reflection is not facing the toilet bowl in the mirror as I am. He's facing me.

I snap my head towards him, and instantly the mirror image is back to normal. A replica Jeremy is standing in front of the toilet staring directly at me as I stare back at him. I'm just imagining things. I think. Aren't I?

Stop it!

There is no way that my reflection was ever not what it's supposed to be.

I look back at the toilet, and inside, a small statuette of an imp floats around in the water. It wasn't there just a second ago. I close my eyes shut, pressing them so tightly that an artificial light forms in their pressure. Then I open them again.

The little imp is still there, revolving around and round on itself, floating about mindlessly. Bending down, looking closer at it, I see that it's a chess piece. A pawn. The same one from my dream.

My hand snaps to the lever, and I flush the toilet without even giving it a thought. The imp swirls around and round and then shoots down through the hole. The water gurgles, and I wait for the water to fill up again. Another statuette comes up from the hole. This time it's a gray creature with bat wings and a devilish smile on its face.

I wait a moment to be able to flush again, and then the creature goes down like the one before it. The water gurgles louder this time. I wait again for the water to rise, but it doesn't.

Then the toilet begins to quiver. The bolts tightening it down to the ground tremble. The trembling increases, and soon the whole toilet resembles a can of paint being shaken by a paint-mixing machine. The back cover falls off and crashes to the ground, cracking in two.

The trembling bolts turn slowly, loosening more and more by the second. Then, water starts to rise again, sloshing around violently. I try to hold the toilet steadily with my arms, but it's useless. My entire upper body shakes along with it.

A deep rumbling emerges from beneath my feet. One by one, the light blue tiles begin to crack in spider web designs, each taking their turn. My hands' grasp tighten around the seat of the toilet, but by now only one bolt is still in place and the whole bowl wobbles extensively. The base of it breaks off and the water dumps out to wet my feet.

A second later, a torpedo of swirling water shoots up to the ceiling from where the bowl had just been, pushing it aside like nothing.

Splashing off the ceiling, the water comes down like shooting rain. Soon the blast of water darkens to the color of feces and other bodily wastes.

The floor tiles begin to push up and grind on one another. Brown water leaks up from the gaps. A wave of roars spreads all around the bathroom walls. Chunks of the ceiling break off in layers, falling to the ground with a mist of white powder.

As all of this is happening, I'm pressed against the far corner of the bathroom by the shower entrance.

The pipe leading up to the bathroom sink jangles. It waves back and forth, too much pressure going through it. Seconds later, the sink faucet explodes. Water bursts out from the hole in a shotgun blast.

There's a *ting* sound that comes from behind me, and I know that the shower glass is about to break along with everything else. I crouch in a ball, stuffing my head between my knees and covering it with my arms. The glass cracks, moments later shattering down into hundreds of different-sized triangles. Some of the glass showers down on me, cutting thin but sharp scratches into my neck and back. The stinging pain is intolerable like damps of alcohol over a massive amount of wounds. I wait for all the glass to fall down before I decide to get up.

I try to stand, with the chunks of glass crunching beneath my shoes, but then the uneven pavement of the ground spurts up in small hills. One of the hills pushes up right from beneath my feet, testing my balance. I grab onto the towel hanger, but it snaps off the wall. I fall to the ground onto my right shoulder, pressing on top of a field of jagged glass. The shards dig into my arm, burning a deep fire up the entire length of it.

I scream. The pain is too much for me not to.

The torpedo of toilet water subsides, and then finally cuts off as if something were clogging its path. A blast of floor tiles shoots out, flying through the air like poker cards being tossed. Then, a huge arm punches through the floor. The arm is tremendously big, about the size of my entire body, and the hand itself is the size of my torso. Its fingernails narrow down to sharp points, each of them sharp enough to pierce right through my chest.

I crawl away, making an effort to avoid the glass spread on the ground. Another hill of tiles spurts up, flipping me around onto my back. Before I can get back up, the huge hand has me by the leg. I try to hang on to the cracks in the floor, but it's useless. The tiles just strip away in my grasp as I'm being dragged by the leg.

It pulls me closer to the hole where the toilet had been earlier, all the while my body smacks from left to right against the humps that have formed.

Then the drainpipe from the sink ruptures out, and a sharp length of the pipe snaps, twirling through the air. The sharp metal end jabs right into the huge arm, sticking into it like a rusted needle searching for a vein. There's a shriek, roaring with a tinny sound that scratches my eardrums. The burly fingers of the monstrous hand twitch, and its hold on my leg releases.

Next to the cracked shower there's a broom, and I grab it. I hold the wooden handle by the very end and swing it down like a hatchet against the burly knuckles of the hand. It takes a few hits before finally the wood splinters, forming sharp wooden dentures at the end of it. I hold the stick like a pole about to be thrust in the dirt, and I drive it through the middle of the hand's back. The large fingers lock up like a permanent claw, each of the fingers incapable of bending or extending anymore.

I run to the door and burst it wide open, almost falling forward in the effort.

"Gammy!" I scream desperately. It's funny how when you're in pain, you always scream someone's name. Even if there's not a thing in the world they can do for you.

"What? What is it?" She comes rushing to the hall. My hands, my neck, and my right arm are all bleeding. My clothes are torn and drenched in water. "Oh dear—what happened?"

"Look." I turn back to the bathroom for her to see for herself. But there's nothing to see other than an ordinary, well-taken-care-of bathroom. The mounds on the ground are gone, the cracks have disappeared, and the huge hand has vanished.

"What am I looking at?" she says, stupefied and confused.

"Didn't you hear the noises—the rumbling?"

"No."

"Nothing?"

"No, Jeremy. I'm sorry. Let's get you bandaged up and taken care of."

Chapter 30

Gammy and I are sitting at the kitchen table. We say grace and then we begin to eat in silence. The dishes in front of us each hold a simple plate of penne with meat sauce. Hot steam dances upward from our plates. I stab at small mouthfuls of pasta, and bring it to my mouth. It still hurts to move. Even stretching my fingers out to grab the parmigiano cheese feels like I'm ripping tendons in my arm. I don't move my neck because it hurts a lot less to bring the fork to my mouth—which still feels like knives carving into and digging into my armpit—than to bring my mouth down to the plate.

The silence in the room is uncomfortable. Our forks scrape the plates, and our lips smack around the food. Each noise sounds like a disturbance to the silence, and that's what makes it even more uneasy. Gammy stands up and walks to the stereo. She shuffles through the column of CDs and then picks one to slide in. A guy's voice starts singing about Jesus, praising him for his love and strength. Then Gammy takes her seat again.

"Do you like it?" Gammy says softly, gesturing to the food..

"It's really good."

My fork clanks against the plate at each stab through the pile of pasta.

"Are you feeling okay, Jeremy? You seem upset."

"I am, Gammy. I really am."

"What's the matter?" As if there's a need to ask. The answer is already too obvious. We are prisoners to our own house, left without contact with the outside world, left without hope other than to see yet another dark day, and constantly being harassed by creatures banging at the walls at night. But there is something else, too.

"I keep seeing things. Things that aren't there."

"Like what, Jeremy?" Her voice strikes like a match of reminiscence, as if she can relate to what I'm saying.

"Like shadows out of the corner of my eyes, somebody else's face when I look in the mirror, or slime coming out of the showerhead when it's only water. And it's not just that. Sometimes I feel somebody tapping on my shoulder, and I turn, and there's nobody there. I can't keep going on like this."

"Don't let it scare you, Jeremy. You must keep strong. Keep praying."

"I've *been* praying. Constantly. Every night. Every time I'm scared. Every time I see things that aren't there! But it doesn't seem to get any better or easier! What's the point? What is all this even for?" At one point in time I knew the answer to that question, but now I'm not so sure what it is anymore.

"To test your strength."

"Why?"

"To see if you're strong enough to resist temptation. All this is about getting accepted into Heaven. There won't be a test any more powerful than this. If we can get through it, that means we can achieve anything!"

"Anything," I repeat in a low whisper.

"Just keep strong Jeremy. We're in this together. If you ever feel too weak to go on, come to me. Prayers are more powerful in unity."

"Thanks, Gammy. That means a lot to me."

"Of course, Jeremy. Don't ever think you're alone in this. We're here to help each other."

I take another bite of pasta. As I swallow, something clings to my throat, making me gag. I feel around my palate with a finger and pinch down on a thin hair. I pull on it, and pull on it, and pull on it. It seems to be going on forever.

At first it looks like one big, long, continuing silver hair, but looking at it closer I notice that it's a long line of small hairs tied to one another by several fine knots. They're dog hair, and they're Romulus'. With a final tug, my throat gags in a disgusting *glagh* sound, and out comes a small lump of hair, all bunched up together.

"What did you put in this pasta?" I ask.

"Just sauce, garlic and ground meat."

My stomach revolts. We've been eating Romulus. There's no doubt in my mind. I know that we burned his body days ago, but this is *his* body ground up in our pasta. I know it.

"I can't eat this, Gammy."

"Why? What's wrong?"

I dangle the long ball of hair from my fingers. Her eyes pinch in, trying to focus on what I'm trying to show her.

"Don't you see this?" I ask her.

"What is it? I don't see anything."

I look at the long string, now slobbered by slick saliva and coated with tomato sauce. Yet, she doesn't see it.

Then the CD starts to skip: "…with your strength, we're armed into battle, to fight Satan—fight Satan—Satan—Satan—Satan—Satan…" Over and over it keeps repeating the word, each time the pitch of its voice getting higher and higher. Then it cuts off, and in an incredibly deep, elongated sound, the voice grovels the word, "Saaayt-annnh."

I jump out of my seat, knocking my chair over, and I push the stop button on the CD player. The sound cuts off, giving me relief.

Then the telephone rings, making me jump twice as hard as the music had made me. I pick it up quickly. Wearily, I ask, "Hello?"

"Jeremy! I can't do this anymore!" The voice on the other end is so shaken that I don't even recognize it. But it's a girl, I can tell that much, and she sounds like she's been crying.

"Jessica?" I ask, unsure.

Then her words just rambled out. "I couldn't get a hold of you for so long. I've been trying to call and call and call, but nobody would answer, and sometimes I would hear voices like voices cackling and laughing at me through the phone. It was so horrible, and I've been crying so much; every night I cry and I think about you a lot and that gives me strength but I'm so scared."

"Jessica, I'm here. Be calm. Don't be scared."

"Oh, Jeremy, I'm so glad I finally got you on the phone." And then her voice breaks down crying. I listen to her voice sob into my ear, and I just wait for her to finish.

After a while, once her sobs die down to just sniffles, I ask, "Feel better?"

"Yes."

"It's been horrible, hasn't it?"

"Yes," she says softly.

"Here too."

"I keep having disgusting, terrible dreams. And my dad, he doesn't seem the same. He's always shaken, and jumpy. And when he's not jumpy he doesn't even respond. At night he talks to himself, and when I asked him about it, he said Mom was in the room with him. He's delusional, and that scares me more than anything else."

"Keep strong, Jessica."

"I try, Jeremy. I try."

"Let's say a prayer together now. How 'bout Our Father?"

"Okay."

I start off the prayer and then her voice starts to repeat my words, softly. After a few phrases, our words unite, and together they carry a stronger tune. Once we're finished, I ask, "Was that okay?"

"Let's do another."

Our second one carries out more volume and strength. I can hear her voice carry more confidence with each spoken word. Soon, our voices become roped with emotion, filled with love towards the prayer we recite. Filled with love towards God. With love for each other. With love despite our fears. Filled with so much of it that by the time we finish with "Amen," my voice chokes midway through the word.

"Ay-men!" she says vibrantly. "Much better now."

"I'm glad." A smile forms on my face. She giggles over the phone, filled with complete joy, breaking through her earlier sobs.

So then we talk for hours. She describes some of her dreams, and the things that she's seen in the past couple of days, but her voice isn't at all scared when she talks, but it is serious. We joke around a little, trying to lighten up one another's mood. We talk about an imaginary future between us that will never be, always enticing one other's strengths.

"I love you," she says once our conversation is over.

"I love you, too, Jessica." And we hang up.

Chapter 31

I'm in my bedroom, submerged in darkness. The only light in the room slips through from under the door, and the numbers on the electronic radio give off a somber green glow. The alarm clock is up on a book shelf on the other side of the room. It's there so that I would be forced to get out of bed to shut it off in the mornings when I still went to school. Where the glows of these two light sources can't reach, an impenetrable blackness fills the room.

I lie on my bed looking up, with my hands behind my head. There's nothing to see really, but I keep my eyes open, thinking. I wonder what's next. It seems that everything that could possibly happen already did. And yet the hits scouring just keep on coming. Somehow each day turns worse than the previous one. Every day I feel strength and hope fleeing from my bones, as if the marrow were being sucked out of them.

I tilt my neck back to see the window. Through it I can make out a tiny slit of the moon. It's a pale orange color, shedding its skin and burrowing itself into the darkness. It weeps for this world while the wind howls outside, whispering plans into the ears of the damned. Or maybe it's the damned that are hissing at the wind.

Then the wind seems to be inside my room, whispering to me. A roll of heat fades up from my feet, like a blanket being brought up to my chin. A warm tingle creeps with it, uncomfortable and prickly. The whisper returns, only now it doesn't sound like the wind, but more like a voice.

"Jeremy," the voice says softly, and soothingly. "Jeh…re…mee…" It's a girl's voice, calling for me in a seductive sigh. I sit up briskly in my bed, kicking back with my legs. I don't say anything at first. I don't want whoever it is to know that I'm in here. Then the voice picks up a playful tone. "Jeremy!"

"Who is it?" I whisper back.

I look by the alarm clock where the green glow illuminates the side of a face dimly. I can see one eye clearly, but the other one fades out, shaded by her face. Then the eyes close, and when they open again both are visible. A toned, green circular glow comes from them, stealing my breath. They're Jessica's eyes.

She takes a step forward. "I've come for you," she says. From the green light I can make out the slim outline of her naked body. The light from underneath the door sets on her bare feet. With a few more softly patted steps, she reaches the foot of my bed. Just then, outside the window the moon brightens to a glistening white. The moonlight reaches my bedroom, and I can see a dim image of Jessica, naked, and ready to pounce on the bed.

"How'd you get in here?" I ask her, a little taken back. I shift back in my bed. The sheets ruffle and fold.

She ignores my question and lifts one leg, placing her knee on the bed. Then she does the same with the other, leaning over on all fours like a cat stalking her prey. Her green eyes stare at me in ecstasy, and I can't bring myself to look away. Her lips form a smile as she takes slow, striding steps closer to me.

Her hands grasp for my button-up shirt, and she rips it open with incredible quickness. Then her fingers begin to massage my body, smothering it with her touch.

"What are you doing?" I push myself back in my bed while trying to get a hold of her hands. She pulls away from my hold on her wrists, and continues to caress my chest and arms.

"Just let me," she says. Her voice comes through as a wisp of seduction.

And I let her. Just like that.

Softly, her lips begin to kiss my belly, my chest, my neck, then up to my face, and finally my mouth. Overpowering me, she pins my hands out to my sides. Then her hands let go of my wrists, but mine stay in place as if they were still being held down.

With her fingertips, she caresses my arms down to my shoulders. Then her fingers glide down my torso, reaching a hold of my pants. She tugs them down to my feet, and then right off, throwing them aside to a far corner of the room.

"I can't do this," I tell her. My voice is quivering, childish, weak. "I just can't."

"Don't resist."

Then her smooth legs straddle my pelvis. By now it's too hard to contain my arousal. Immediately, she begins rock on top of me. In my mind I am not here. I am so far away that I can't even control my own body. I feel like I am watching and feeling her through somebody else's skin and bundles of nerves.

"Oh, Jeremy," she moans. She giggles, and then bites down on her lip.

"I can't do this, I can't—I can't—I can't..."

Then she grabs my hands, and cups them to her chest. She squeezes on my fingers, and so my fingers squeeze on her. I'm not controlling my body, she is. I'm helpless. Aren't I? I'm helpless!

Physically this feels so right, but I *know* it's wrong. I know it. I don't want to do this. In my mind I want her off of me.

The spirit is willing but the body is weak.

The phrase just drops in my head, although I don't remember where it is that I heard it. It seems unimportant at the moment, so I put it aside in the back of my head.

I look away, closing my eyes, shutting them so tightly that a blur of white haze drapes over them. I just don't want to look at what I'm doing. I can't look at myself this way.

But my hands keep on squeezing, and Jessica keeps on moaning, each time louder and louder. What if Gammy hears us? How could I bear her seeing me like this?

"Oh,Jeremy! Mmmmm! Oooh...Oh, Jeremy! Mmmmm..."

Then she begins touching my body again. She smothers me in kisses all around my face, nibbling on the soft parts of my skin.

I open my eyes to look up at her, and it's not Jessica that I see. Her eyes are no longer green; they're gray. Her skin has become pasty. Her hair is raggier, and her lips have transformed thin and crisp rather than full and round. Jessica's been replaced by Megan, my ex whom I thought I finally gotten rid of. And yet I don't stop myself, nor her. Megan giggles at me. "Oh, Jeremy! This is so fun." She keeps on riding me, and my hands keep on squeezing. I can't stop! I'm so pathetic that I can't stop.

Only that's a lie. It's not that I can't, it's that I *won't*. I'm caught in the moment, moving along, mimicking Megan's motions. I shut my eyes once again, imagining that it's not Megan who's on top of me but still Jessica.

The moans turn into aggressive, sexual grunts. Each grunt is followed by a heavy breath hushing down over me.

"Com'on, Jeremy! Get into this." And then she laughs. It's a hideous, mocking laughter still filled with sexual enthusiasm.

Oh God, help me, I can't do this!

"Come on! Oh yes, yes, yes!"

Oh God!

"Oh, Jeremy!!!"

Oh-God-oh-God-oh-God-oh-God…

Then, once again I open my eyes. Megan has been replaced by a hideous, bald creature with reptile skin covering her body. The creature hisses at me. Her fangs open wide, and then she cackles horribly into my face. Her pallid, yellow eyes burrow a stare into mine.

Immediately, my arousal cuts off. My hands pull away from her chest. The creature's grin is as wide as her face. She pushes her weight back on her shins, and then curls it onto her toes, elevating herself a few feet above my body. Her hands pull back to her chest, with her fingers spread open, ready to strike.

Before she can pounce on me, I bend my legs, bringing my knees to my chest. Then my feet buck forwards, slamming on the creature's torso. She snags back, and her body is launched over my bed and across the room where she raps hard against my desk.

She hisses hideously, with her yellow eyes still visible in the darkness. I roll off the bed and spring to the lamp switch. I flick it on, and it takes a few seconds for my eyes to adjust to the light. When I finally open them again, the creature's gone. She's disappeared from my room.

I pick up my shorts and pants and slip them back on. I plant my face into my hands in self-humiliation, knowing that I've allowed a demon to enter the house.

Chapter 32

All the clocks have stopped working properly. Some rest at a standstill, others have begun ticking backwards, while the rest give different times.

A message written on the fogged kitchen window reads: Tick Tock. Stops the clock. Then your minds will soon unhinge. As desires fill thy binge.

The words are written on the outside of the window, impossible for me to wipe off. When will all this be over? How many more times will I be tempted, and how many will I fail?

It was Jessica who was in my room last night, but then she turned into a monster. I wonder if the same happened in her room. I wonder if *my* image came to her, tempting her with something she couldn't resist.

Before I can talk to Gammy about any of this, I *have* talk to Jessica and find out if it was the same for her. Why, I don't know. But I know that I need to talk to her.

I pick up the phone to my ear, and a raspy voice whispers, "Wicked! Wicked! How easily you fall!"

I slam the receiver back in its cradle, and I pick it up again. The voice is gone, and a dial tone hums a ring in its place. I dial Jessica's number and begin to count the rings. It takes twelve before a shaky voices asks abruptly, "Who is this?"

"Mr. Davis, this is Jeremy. Could I speak with Jessica?"

"I know about you! You're trying to take her away. But I won't let you!"

"Take her away...?"

"She came to you last night, didn't she?"

"How did you—"

"She came to you, yes. I know very well. And you took advantage of her." His voice sounds insidious, like the voice of a man plotting something.

"Mr. Davis, you don't understand. You don't know what really came to tempt—"

"Tempt?" he says furiously. "Tempt you say! You *raped* her! She came to you, and you assaulted her, violating her body!"

"Raped her?" My voice is quivering. What is he thinking?

"Oh, don't you play dummy with me! I know all too well. He told me *everything!*"

"Who?"

"But that's all right. That's all right." His voice is more tamed now, relaxed and drugged. "I know that it wasn't my Jessica after all. Oh, how stupid you must have felt! How *stupid!*"

"Listen, Mr. Davis, I didn't rape anyone."

"She was only a seductive dancer of the night, after all. She came to offer you a dance, but that wasn't enough for you, was it?"

"It wasn't like that."

"So you pounced on her, Jeremiah, because you wanted *more!* The dance was not enough for your desires."

Then your mind will soon unhinge, as desires fill thy binge

"She came to me! She came *onto* me!" I say, pleading him to believe me.

"That's not the way *he* told the story."

"He? Who's *he*?"

"Oh, you know well who *he* is. The man in the black suit and red suede shoes. The man who sent the dancing girl to you. He says you know him well." His voice is cool, each word flowing out smoothly in a sedative roll.

"I don't know who you're talking about."

"No matter. The joke was on you after all."

"Could you please put Jessica on the phone?"

"*NO!*" The word blares into my ear, sounding sore and contempt with rage.

"Why won't you let me talk to her?"

"You're not going to take her away from me! I won't let you! She's *my* daughter."

"Please, just—"

I hear his receiver slamming down, cutting off our conversation. The line falls dead, filled by silence. Then a breath rises through the receiver to reach my ear, and I slam it down on its cradle.

Chapter 33

After dinner, I go back to my room. Gammy and I passed the entire time in silence. In my mind I kept arguing with myself whether I should tell her about what happened in my bedroom last night or not. Finally, by the time dinner was over, I settled on not.

As I step in, I decide to leave the door ajar.

"Close the door if you will," a charmed voice tells me, taking me by surprise. I turn on the light, and a man comes into view. He stands lean and tall, looking at me with his hands joined in front of him. "Go on," he says, waving a hand at me to shut the door.

I close it firmly with a click and then turn back to the man. His face is brilliant, full of blush. His hair, tainted orange and messy, looks as if it was slicked up with gel and then fussed by the wind. Two pointy sideburns curve downward in front of his ears, touching his jaw line. A thin, blond beard surrounds his lips, reaching around to his pointy chin.

A smile arises on his face, and his eye ablaze with vigor, looking intensely at me.

"Who are you?" I ask immediately.

"What, no hello? No 'How you been?' 'How's it going?'"

"You were in my dream," I realize, thinking out loud.

"How nice of you to remember. Only, I look a lot better without all the blubber and fat on my belly, don't you think?"

"What are you doing here?" I ask accusingly.

"Well, I'm certainly not here to play chess, as you can see. I've forgotten my bag. Maybe some other time. I'm here to take you back, Jeremy. To be friends again. For old time's sake." He says this while spreading his hands out to the sides, palms open, and standing on the tip of his toes, making a quick up-and-down motion. On his feet he wears a pair of red suede shoes.

"We were never friends," I say bitterly.

"No? Then who provided all the fun you've had over the past years? The drugs, the booze, the sex? It was me, my young friend. Every time you wanted to get wasted, bam! I put a bottle in your hand. Every time your dick was so hard that it could take you out for a walk? Bam! I found a nice girl for you to play with."

"I don't need any of it any more."

"Are you so sure?"

"Yes!"

"Then what about last night, Jeremy? Didn't you take the girl I sent to you?"

"I thought she was Jessica!" I say defensively.

"What difference does it make?" He pauses for a moment, waiting for an answer, but I don't have one to give. "Besides, it's the act that counts. Isn't that right? Would you have acted any differently if you *knew* it wasn't Jessica, or if she hadn't been the one coming onto you?"

"Yes."

"Don't lie to me, Jeremy. And don't lie to yourself! The fact of the matter is that you let my girl jump your bones, lickety-split between her legs, and that is all that counts. The girl came, and you welcomed her. So maybe, I'm thinking, you need me after all. Which works out perfectly because I need you as well."

"I don't need you."

"Don't argue with me, Jeremy," he says impatiently. "And just listen…"

"How did you get in here?"

"Would you quit interrupting?" he says angrily, but then, more calmly as if stretching his breath with patience, he says, "But if you must know, you *let* me in. Well actually, I'm not here at all. Not in the physical sense, no. I'm inside your head. You're picturing me, and I look exactly the way you want me to appear, from head to toes. Even these shoes. They're on my feet only because poor Mr. Davis mentioned them to you, and that image got stuck in your head. Didn't it?"

"You're not in my head. I can see you! I'm not delusional."

"Really! You think so? Go ahead and pull out a tape recorder. Top shelf behind you, between the picture of your parents and the one of Jessica. Record my voice, if you like. Or ask your Gammy to come in and take a look at me. Go ahead! The only thing you'll get on that tape is the howl of the wind outside. If Gammy were to listen in on our conversation, the only thing she would hear would be your voice.

"So," he continues, but pauses for a moment to remember what it is that he was going to say. "Ah, yes. To answer your question, I'm here with your own consent. You gave me an all-access pass the moment you allowed Jessica to hop on your bed. And *that* was good enough for the 'Good Ol' Man Upstairs' to grant me the same permission. Nothing gets done without having it run by Him first, of course. Nothing.

"Anyways, before we get to the business part of our meeting, I'd like to congratulate you."

"What for?" I say, displeased that he would grant me such praise.

"For defeating my small, yet very untamed, army; the one led by my boy Crandall." It takes me a moment to realize what he's talking about. I think back to Ben's death. My fingers clutch at my pant legs. He continues, "That was truly magnificent, I must say. Quite a show, really. You just incinerated them all without even an effort."

"I didn't do anything. God is the one who destroyed them, not me."

"How *typical* of a 'true' Christian. How naïve! Always giving *Him* all the credit. And for what? What about all the things *you've* accomplished?"

"I can't do anything without God. I realize that now."

"How weak. And you're so ready to admit that? For what? What do *you* get in return? It surprises me why He doesn't just wipe you all off the face of the Earth and start over from scratch. Oh, but oops, that's exactly what He's doing. And maybe this time He'll place the tree a bit more out of reach."

"What are you talking about?" I ask curiously despite my deep disgust for him, listening carefully.

"Think about it. It took Adam and Eve less time to ruin God's plan than it took Him to put it together! He had warned them, too! He promised them death if they dared taste the fruit, but they did anyways. And then what happened? Did they die? No. Of course not. He went back on His word. He couldn't possibly kill Adam and Eve just days after creating them. That would have been fruitless. It would mean that God created a mistake." His words come out crisply, full of delight for the story he is telling me.

"So then he waited," he says with a wide grin and narrowing eyes. "And all for nothing. For thousands and thousands of years he watched men kill one another, steal from each other, rape women, submit themselves to false gods, and even live their lives thankless of Him. He was displeased by all this. He has been for many years. So finally his patience ran out, and He decides to do something about it. And what *is* that something?" He pauses, waiting to see if I can form my own answer, then says, "To *wipe out* the world of course. But then again, He needs to put a twist on it, or else He'll have committed an even greater mistake for waiting so long.

"So the twist is, 'You will be tested!' He doesn't say, 'If you pass you will remain alive,' no. He says, 'Those of you who pass shall enter My Kingdom.' Everyone dies, Jeremy. Everyone. Even the good, and the just, and the righteous. Even you. He wants to completely wipe your sorry asses off the face of this Earth! Now, does *that* seem like a just and fair God to you? Does it seem right that, just because *He* was the one who committed the mistake, the population of the entire world has to pay for it? No, I say. It doesn't.

"He wants to start from scratch, and has found a way to do so without admitting His mistake. The mistake of creation. But you see, He is so *fixated* on creating the perfect humanity that he *has* to do this. And so He waited, and waited, and waited. Then finally, you were born, and you were quite the lottery ticket, let me tell you. Say, Jeremy, do you *know* why you were chosen?"

"Yes."

"Why is it, then?"

"Because I'm important to him, just like any other man or woman is important to Him. He wanted to show it to me personally."

"Wrong. Don't make me laugh, Jeremy. Don't compare yourself to just any other ordinary man. Do you remember how you felt after waking up that day in church?"

"I felt nauseated," I say solemnly, "like my intestines were rotting inside of me."

"Is that all? Just some mere rotting nausea, and that's it? You see, Jeremy, *that's* why you were chosen. There have been men in the history of the Earth whose eardrums exploded just by listening to the true voice of God. It's *immense* in its power! Other men have become blind after seeing his true image. But you. You actually *felt* God inside of you. You were breathing God! And you got away with some mere nausea? Who else could withstand that? *That,* my friend, is why you were selected among the billions. You are a rare case, Jeremy, and that's why I'm here."

"Why do it that way? Why possess a human body to speak through instead of sending a messenger?"

"We live in the age of disbelief, Jeremy. There's too much chaos out there, too much corruption, for so many to believe in what is spiritual. How many would listen if any ordinary man came out and announced, 'Listen to what God has said to me'? No, not so many. People need to see to believe, or at least know that there exist those who saw with their own eyes. A third-person narrative doesn't quite cut the cheese."

"So what do you want from me?"

"Just bare with me for a moment. You were picked...and then you were used. He needed you to carry his message so that regular ears could hear Him. Then, once that was over with, all is done and all is forgotten. He used you once and then left you on the road, discarded like a condom. And for what? All done to glorify *Himself.* How selfish of Him.

"But if you join me, Jeremy, the glory will be *ours.* We'll share it. Together! You've got some talents in you, ma'boy. I've seen it. I've seen what you can do. I know what you can withstand. Your body is filled to the brim with powers you don't even know about. We can be a team. Partners, if you prefer. You have what I need: A body to endure the impact of my strength carried through it. Together we can rule the entire world. Life as we know it doesn't have to end once Judgment is over. With us in control, we can keep the Earth and all those still living upon it. What do you say?"

He smiles broadly, waiting for my response.

"You disgust me," I finally answer.

"Oh, don't talk like that, Jeremy. Don't tell me about disgust and sickly shit that makes you go vomit. You want this to be over, don't you? To be a thing of the past? I can end it all at the blink of an eye. Don't go on to fulfill God's selfishness."

"How can you call God selfish? He's done everything for His people. He gave us *life*. He put us into existence. You say He's forgotten me, but ever since I carried His message He's been with me every step of the way. He didn't abandon me once. You don't fool me with your lies. You told Mr. Davis that I raped his daughter, and he believed you. It was lies to him then, and it's lies to me now. If you take over my body, I won't even exist anymore. I'll have fallen into a coma that I may never get out of!"

"Come on, Jeremy," he tries to reason with me, his temper quickly bubbling. "Do you really want to be responsible for the death of six and a half *billion* people? The entire world?"

"You know what you are? Greedy. You want it all, don't you? Well, that's too much. I can't let you have it."

"You're making a grave mistake," he says, churning his words into a threat between his curling lips.

"No. I've already committed enough of those, but now comes the time to end them. I've got to redeem myself."

"Redemption? Is that what you think you're gaining by sending me away?"

"Get out of my room, Satan."

"I can make things harder on you if I wish. *Much* harder than they have been so far," he says, rasping angrily.

"I'll be waiting then."

"Jeremy. Think again!" he snarls, but already he's begun to disintegrate like a statue made of dust. Fading…fading…and then gone with a final yell that echoes through my room.

Chapter 34

I'm in the living room, reciting the rosary with Gammy.

"That won't help you any," a voice rasps into my ear.

Gammy keeps praying, unfazed. "Did you hear that?" I say, stopping her for a moment.

"Hear what?"

"No, never mind…keep going." Then a strained chuckle follows. Gammy doesn't seem to be hearing it, so I dismiss it.

"Je…reh…meee…Oh…Je…reh…meee…" the voice taunts inside my head. My jaws lock tightly, and I desperately try to block it out, jaws clenched and tongue clamped to my palate.

Then a sharp pang of pain bolts through my chest, knocking me back on the couch. Gammy looks at me. "What's wrong?" she asks, worried.

But I can't speak. The jolt knocked the wind out of me, and now I struggle with breathing. I gasp, but no air flows into my mouth, and my throat makes odd, squeaky noises with each breath. I pat myself on the chest, but it doesn't help.

Gammy sets her rosary down and approaches me on the couch. "Jeremy, what's wrong?"

Come on, Jeremy, why won't you answer your grandma? She's only trying to help, the voice mocks me with ridiculous joy.

I cough up a huge burst of air, exhaling. Then I take in a deep breath, and I can feel my face getting red and my eyes watery.

"I couldn't breathe," I tell Gammy, still panting heavily.

"Are you all right, now?"

"I think so."

No you're not! the voice screams at me with a maniacal laugh. Suddenly, I'm thrust off the couch and flung onto the coffee table, knocking it over. My side hits the edge of it, inflicting a jab of pain against my ribs. The coffee on top of the table splashes on the ground, staining the carpet. Gammy jumps back in her seat, gasping, shocked by what just happened.

How did you like that, Jeremy? You want some more, don't you?

"No, stop!"

But the voice won't listen. My body is shot back against the wall like a rock from a slingshot. The impact makes me cough out all the air in my lungs, leaving me breathless. My back burrows into the wall, and I can feel the thin layer of plaster crumbling around me. I wheeze for air, reaching out for whatever I can grasp.

What's the matter? You don't like flying anymore?

Then my back slides up against the wall, slamming my head into the ceiling. Blood trickles out of my skull, reaching around my face to my nose and lips. My body is pushed harder and harder upward, straining my neck and back with pressure.

I told you that you should have joined me!

"Get out of my body, Satan!" I scream, struggling to get the words out.

I'm not in your body. If I were, none of this would be happening. I'm all around you! Can't you feel me? Can't you smell my aroma?

The stench of rotten cottage cheese infiltrates my nose with the huff of a breath.

Sweet like roses, isn't it?

"Stop it! Enough!" I scream with my chin digging into my chest. Then to Gammy I yell, "Help me! Do something! Please!"

She can't help you, Jeremy. Only you can help yourself. Join me, and all this can end right now.

"No!"

As you wish.

Then I'm slammed on the ground onto my knees and elbows. From the far corner of the room, I can hear Gammy whimpering and giving out screams of fear. Why isn't she doing anything?

What could she do! Hug you and kiss you until the pain goes away? The laughter that follows rings into my ears, echoing inside my head like a scream shouted into a coffee can.

On the ground, I'm flipped over onto my back and dragged by my neck and shoulders. My body is pulled and yanked in all different directions, sideswiping chairs and objects in the way, knocking them over. My legs swing around, kicking a stand with a glass vase on top of it. Then I'm spun around quickly, and my head clashes against the vase. The water splashes on me, but the vase doesn't break. Already, I can feel the bruises forming all over my body on top of the ones I've already got

Then the grip on my neck lets go and gets hold of my feet instead. As I'm being dragged, my shirt lifts up, and the carpet rubs hard against my bare back, scraping burns into my skin.

"Why are you doing this?"

Because I'm loving it too much!

"Love?" The way he used the word disgusts me. "What do you know about love? Love is affection and caring and compassion. All *you* have to offer is rage and suffering and hate!" I say all this in thought, being in too much pain to speak with my voice.

Oh, I know plenty about love! I know that love is deception!

"Love can only exist through God."

Exactly my point! You're being deceived! How can you have love towards Him when, as we speak, you feel terrible pain? Are you sure you know what love is? Tell me, Jeremy, what is truth? What is sanctity? What is faith? Hope? Spirituality? Forgiveness?

My head is banged against the corner of the wall with each question, tormenting me with repetitive slashes of pain.

"You're trying to confuse me!"

Am I? What is the point?

"Stop it! I don't know what the point is!"

Deception! That's what the point is! I'm not the only tailor of such a trait. He is the master of it!

"Enough! I can't take it anymore!"

Tell me, Jeremy, who is allowing this suffering?

"You are!"

Sure, I'm causing it, but am I allowing it?

I'm flipped over again, and my cheek is pushed against the floor, pressing back and forth into the rug. It feels like sandpaper tearing at my face.

"I am! *I'm* allowing it!"

Wrong, Jeremy! Then my face is slammed nose first into the wall. A spider web of fogged pain shoots up my nose, surrounding my eyes, stinging like hundreds of needle pricks.

God is allowing it! Seems to me that you've been deceived by him, haven't you? You're blaming yourself for His doing!

"If that is His will, then it's my will to accept it!"

To accept pain?

"Yes."

Just moments ago you begged me to stop! You implored me! Why the sudden change?

Then I'm slid into the kitchen. My legs squeak against the tiled flooring. I look up over my shoulders, and I see a kitchen drawer slide open. In it, I hear the silverware stirring. I'm pulled towards the opened drawer, and my head is lifted just above it so that I can look in. Forks and knives are dispersed messily everywhere with corkscrews, a can opener, and several other blades.

Let's play surgeon, shall we? I'm going to dunk your face in, and we'll see what comes out of it. Any objections?

"None."

What? Satan says, confused. My face reaches over the drawer, looking down from above the mixed silverware. *You're not going to beg me to stop?*

"No."

Why?

"It's what you said. God is allowing this pain, and I am a subject of God. If he allows it, then I will too. Let the pain come. Let my love for God show!"

The hold on me drops. My chin smacks against the wooden drawer, and then I fall to the ground, unsupported. No silverware falls out, and the drawer remains stable, leaning out over my head. I lay down with all my energy drained. I breathe in and out. I close my eyes, feeling too tired to move.

I've won over Satan's test. I realize that now.

Then I hear Gammy scream, "Jeremy! Help!" Her voice sounds muffled, as if covered by a mountain of pillows. I sit up at the sound of her scream and rush back to the living room as fast as I can where chairs, lampshades, and everything else is knocked over or turned upside down.

"Where are you?" I shout, not seeing her anywhere.

"Over here! Under the sofa."

The large couch is turned over, and underneath I see Gammy's face peeking through the gap. I step in front of the sofa and bend down to grab the back of it. My fingers tighten around the back's edge, but my muscles feel tired, too weak to even budge it an inch. My vision blurs and fades to an opaque gray. I shake my head violently, snapping back into focus. I lift the couch, and with a single swoop it flips back on its legs. Gammy crawls out, and I flop down on the sofa.

All the shapes in front of my eyes turn to opaque blobs, too blurry to make anything out. Darkness follows, and I crumble beneath unconsciousness.

Chapter 35

I open my eyes, and Gammy's face gently fades into view. She's looking down on me. I look around and see that I'm still in the living room, lying on the sofa. Gammy's lips form a sweet smile.

"Are you feeling any better?" she asks, handing me a glass of water with ice cubes melting inside of it.

"Yeah. I think so." I try to sit up, but I stop halfway, slumping back down without enough strength to support me.

"Just lay there awhile. You still need your strength." She feeds small oval pills into my mouth, saying, "Take these. They're aspirins." She supports my neck with her hand as I take a deep gulp of water.

"How long was I out for?"

"Not sure. The clocks still aren't working. I'm guessing a good few hours."

"Did anything happen while I was asleep?"

"Not a thing," she says blissfully, "It was quiet the whole time, and I enjoyed every second of it. I cleaned up all your cuts and bruises."

"Along with the living room, I noticed." I touch around on my face and feel bandages covering my nose, cheeks and forehead.

"You looked like a mess when you passed out," Gammy says with a caring expression on her face, "but it's not so bad now that you're all cleaned up."

"Thanks, Gammy."

"You know, ever since you were a little boy, you always managed a way to get into bad scrapes. I remember one time, your mother invited me over for Trevor's birthday dinner and you were out back playing with Spot…"

"Spot?" I ask, confused.

"Spot was your first dog. You were only three or four at the time. And anyway, you must have been trying to ride him in the back yard and fell a few times because when you came in, all ready for dinner, you had cuts and bruises all over you. But you were laughing! I couldn't believe it. You were smiling and prancing around like you just had the time of your life! You didn't even cry when Barbara cleaned you up with the hydrogen peroxide."

"That stuff stings," I comment.

"I was amazed. So unlike your own dad! When Trevor was little, he wasn't like that at all." She laughs softly for a moment, reminiscing over her youthful mother years. "He'd make a scene over the slightest scratch."

"So *that's* why he was such a pacifist!" I say humorously.

"Oh no." Gammy laughs joyfully. "Your father was no wimp, I can tell you that much. He was a pacifist because he was damn good at it. It's what he did best. He's gotten himself out of some really tough situations. Did you know that he was held at gun point one time?"

"Really!"

"Yes. But this was before you were born. He must have been twenty or so. He came home telling me about it like it was nothing at all. He was at the bank and two men came in to rob it. They told everyone to get down on the ground, but Trevor refused. The two men started shouting at him, but your father kept quiet, looking at the air and around as if he were deaf and mute to the world. They put their guns to his head, but he just stood there. I forget all the details, but I remember what Trevor said to one of the two men."

"What did he say?"

"'Your mother is watching you from Heaven, and she's crying for you because of this.'"

"How did he know that his mother was dead? Was he just guessing?" I ask.

"Oh no, not a guess at all. Trevor said that an angel whispered it into his ear. He even knew her name, but I forget it now. Then he told me that the robber broke down crying. Instantly. Like the switch of a light. Trevor comforted him, and then they walked out together. They went for coffee to talk things over."

"Just like that?" I say, incredulously.

"Just like that. I didn't believe it either the first time I heard it. But then he told his dad, and his friends, and anybody he got a chance to."

"What about the other robber? He didn't try to stop them or anything?"

"He must have been too shocked to do anything when he saw his partner crying. He didn't even finish robbing the bank afterwards. He backed down because his partner walked out with Trevor."

"Wow. That's pretty amazing. What did Dad and the robber talk about?"

"Life, God, religion…things like that. They became good friends after that."

"They did? That's incredible. How come Dad never told me about this?"

"You know the man. You've met him before," Gammy says plainly.

"Who? The robber?"

"After that day he met Trevor, he dedicated his life to God and to the Church. He studied to become a priest, and years later he became the parish priest of St. Regis' Church."

"Father Birmingham was the *robber!*" I say, unbelievingly.

"That's right."

Chapter 36

"God, I miss Mom and Dad *so* much," I say finally after thinking over the story.

"I know, Jeremy. It's hard." She puts her hand around my shoulders. By now I've regained my strength and I'm sitting up.

I start to cry. Tears flow from my eyes and curve over my lips. It's been too long since I've cried for them. I remember how every time they came to mind, I would just fall into silence. Even during the funeral, my eyes were tearless. I held my clasped hands together, neck tilted forward and my head slumped towards the ground. But my face kept dry while everyone else's didn't.

"I still don't understand why they had to die. How could Dad survive a robbery but not a couple of bums off the street?"

Gammy pulls me closer to her, hugging me tighter, gently putting a hand to my cheek. "Shh, honey. We can't change the past."

"I wish they were still alive!" I scream painfully, backing away from Gammy's grasp. "Why can't you bring them back, God! Why!"

"It doesn't work that way, Jeremy," Gammy says softly, trying to comfort me.

"Why not? If God can make me levitate in the air, make thousands of people vanish at the sound of a scream, and can even lock the entire world inside their houses for forty days, then why can't he bring two persons back to life!"

"What would be the point?" she says calmly. "This Judgment will determine the end of all that is living. You'll see them soon enough, Jeremy. Don't worry."

"But I want to see them *now*. I need them so bad."

"Jeremy." Gammy leans closer to me, trying to hold me in her arms. Just then, the doorbell rings.

"What was that?" Gammy turns around shocked.

"The doorbell," I say dazed, merging between a statement and a question.

Gammy looks back at me, her eyes quivering. "We don't have a doorbell."

The bell rings again, and the sound fills my mind with recollections from the past. That sound! It's so familiar. But from where? It draws me back to my childhood, and suddenly I remember. My parents' doorbell had always reminded me of water drops plopping. This is that doorbell.

They've come back.

"It's Mom and Dad!" I tell Gammy joyfully. I jump from the couch onto my feet.

"No, Jeremy!" Gammy grabs a hold of my wrist tightly. Her eyes pleading me with an expression I don't understand. "Don't answer that door."

"But it's *them*!" I shout down at her with a tone mixed with joy and contempt towards her for trying to stop me. I yank my wrist out of her hold, and step closer to the sound of the bell ringing again.

Gammy tugs at my shirt with a clutched fist.

"Gammy! Stop it! Don't you get it? It's them!" I pull away again, but she dives for my legs, claming them tightly together. I try to slip a foot out, but my legs buckle. I lose my balance and fall to the ground hard, taking Gammy down with me.

"Don't answer that door!" Gammy pleads from below my knees, through groans of pain.

"I've got to!" I say, hurt by her demand. "You were wrong, Gammy! They *can* come back! They *are* back!"

"It's not *them*!"

"But it is! It has to be!" I shout at her angrily. I jerk my legs to get her hold loose, and then I scramble onto my hands and knees. The doorbell stops ringing. "Mom! Dad?" I shout for them in hope.

Silence answers my call.

No! Please don't be gone already! So quickly? They rang the bell only three times!

"Jeremy!" A sweet angelical voice calls for me from outside the door. "Mom?"

"Yes, honey! It's us! Come let us in." Her voice soothes my ears, grasping me away with her call. Her voice. It's just as I remembered it. Just how she sounded in my dreams.

"Mom! Dad! It's really you!"

"Jeremy! It's *not* them!" Gammy shouts. I pause and turn only to watch her struggle with herself on the floor, but then I turn away again, leaving her without aid. If I help her up, she'll try to stop me again.

"Come on, Jeremy. It's dark outside. Let us in," Mom says.

"Where's Dad?" I ask. I need to hear his voice to assure me that it's them.

"I'm right here," he says. Just the sound of his voice makes my chest crumble with softness. "I'm not going anywhere, don't worry."

Far behind me, Gammy is still groaning in pain trying to get up. "Come help me, Jeremy, please!" she begs me.

"Come answer the door. Don't you want to see us!" my father calls louder over Gammy's cries. Tears of joy flow out in streams from my eyes, wetting my face and the bandages over my cuts.

I press my face to the door, peeking into the peephole. Through it, I can see two obscure figures in front of a deep, dark black sky. "I can't really see you. It's too blurry," I say with my face stretched with a smile and my eyes pouring out tears.

"That's all right," Mom says, laughing, "Open up and you will."

I begin to unlatch the locks. "You remember when I was so small that I couldn't even get up to the peephole, and you had to lift me, Dad?" I say, as I pull on the chain latch. My hands tremble from all the excitement.

"Of course I remember. You were so small."

I reach for my keys to unlock the bolt above the doorknob. I slide a key in, but the knob won't turn. I flip through the rest, and finally find the right one. I slide it in, ready to turn.

"All right, enough with the wait, Jeremy!" Dad shouts at me. "Open this fucking door!"

"Dad?" I ask confused.

"Your dad didn't mean that, Jeremy. Come on, let us in!" Mom tries to keep her voice cheerful, but I sense a hint of annoyance as she speaks the last phrase.

Then a woman's voice speaks to me in my mind. It's a voice I've heard before, just days prior to the beginning of Judgment. *Don't be fooled by the sounds and images you know cannot exist*, the voice says.

"Open the door, Jeremy!" the voice of my mom shouts, tainted by anger. "Open it *now!*"

I pull the key out. A shiver shoots up my arm, tingling it with dread.

"Open it!" they start screaming together.

I turn away, and walk back to Gammy. My knees give and I fall to my chins so hard that I feel like I've crashed down from the ceiling. I kneel beside her, and hold her shoulders tightly against me. "It's not them?" I ask, still needing to be convinced.

"No, Jeremy. It's not."

And I start crying again, but the tears are painful this time around.

Chapter 37

Hours have passed since the doorbell first rang through the house. The voices impersonating my parents are long gone, giving up on any chance of coming inside. I can't believe how close I came to opening that door. If I hadn't hesitated just long enough, it would have all been over. All the effort we put into these days would've ended in ruin. I can't even begin to imagine what it would be like to live in this house for the rest of eternity. I escaped such a fate by a mere slip of the key.

Worse yet, I could've compromised the same fate for Gammy.

My train of thought is broken up when I hear the tick of a clock. I look up. Above the stove in the kitchen, the hands of the clock just moved for the first time in days. Looking at the arrows, I see that they point to four o'clock.

I look at my wristwatch, a digital. Every day until now it showed meaningless lines that didn't even form numbers. But now that I look at it, I see that it flashes 4:0.

"Gammy! Look at the clocks! They're all the same!"

"Better yet!" she says, unable to maintain her own excitement. "Look outside!"

It can't be. The windows are no longer filled by darkness. There's light that shines through! The light is so bright that it hurts my eyes to even look, and I have to squint them to enjoy it. It's pure white. It's as white as the lack of all shadows and darkness, all eliminated from it.

"It's over," I say breathlessly, filled over the brim with emotions that I can't even begin to describe. I feel like I'm being born again!

"It's time for us to finally leave the house," Gammy says, holding my hand firmly.

As we approach the front door, my heart beats rapidly, drumming away with vigor. I unlock the last bolt on the door and place my hand over the doorknob. Gammy puts hers over mine. Slowly, we turn the knob together. The hinges squeak, and the door swings open.

Outside, the shapes of houses, trees, and everything else are bleached by the bright light. It comes through from every direction. It's impossible to shade my eyes from it, but now it's also become less painful to bear. Then, as it becomes brighter and brighter, a sense of need for it overfills me. I depend, stand, and live for this light.

More and more people step outside. Then the landscape around us disappears and the houses vanish, allowing me to see for miles in every direction. People are sparsely scattered all around us.

Then a deep voice rumbles within me, coating my ears, face, and mind with its sound. The very first wisp of sound comes through as powerful as a bullhorn, shaking my soul within the boundaries of my skin. It doesn't speak in a language that forms words, but in a message that has meaning. I can hear it, and I can understand it, and yet, it's a language I've never heard before.

The voice says, *Now comes the time for you to view your life as I've seen it.* Everyone listens, each one of us being spoken to individually. *From beginning to now, these are your joys and all that has pleased Me.*

Suddenly, all the pleasures of life rush in like a waterfall trying to fill a single bucket. The smell of the first breath of life I ever took surges through my nostrils. The feel of warmth and love soothes into my heart. The taste of cranberry Kool-Aid tickles my tongue. Flowers bloom within my chest, and I can feel it being lifted higher than anyone has ever reached. Compassion strokes my cheeks with a gentle touch. My love for my parents grazes my chin. My lips tighten with a puckered kiss. The sound of nature calling the morning to rise calms my ears. The sight of vibrant colors blankets over my eyes. And the touch of wool envelops my skin.

Oh such joy! Such passion! Such fulfillment!

Then the voice speaks again, this time in a saddened tone. *And from beginning to now, here are your sins as I've seen them. These are the things that have displeased Me.*

The bright, flashy colors fade, replaced by a murky maroon fog that clots everything up. A deep pain rushes down my throat, eyes, nose, and ears, seeping through my skin, burrowing into me from every direction like snakes digging through sand. My eyes water and flinch at the first scent of my sins. But then the scent becomes stronger, more pungent. The sins intertwine and enlarge, expanding and twisting with one another inside my physical body.

Hate. Disgust. Contempt. Violence. Lies. Deception. Sorrow. Anger. Lust. Regret ...

They all accumulate, toppling over one another, slowly melting and blending together as one. It's like black mud dripping down to form layers upon layers of insufferable pain and sorrow. My eyes are pressed shut, too heavy with the glue of sin to remain open.

Jealousy. Greed. Corruption. Selfishness. Pride. Impatience. Vanity. Revenge. Intolerance. Rage...

Heat intensifies in me, burning all over. And just when I can't bear it any longer, more and more fills in, roaring through my body like lava burning down houses and trees to the ground. My closed eyelids are the screens onto which my life is projected. They've become canvases filled with self-pity, all which my eyes can't help but keep looking into.

Finally the pain ends, and when my eyes open, I find myself hunched down on the ground with saliva streaming out of my screaming lips. Now I understand. This was the pain I've caused God all of my life. This was the damage that has slowly corroded my soul over the past nine years. This, I've finally left behind.

Now is when it all ends, the Voice says. *Now is the start of a new beginning. For everyone. For everything.*

A circle forms on the ground, silver against the rest of the whiteness. One by one, the souls of people step into the circle and disappear, leaving their bodies behind. Gammy goes in front of me, vanishing like the rest.

As I step towards the circle, more and more voices make themselves heard by my ears. I hear Jessica laughing with her father, calling out for my name. With them are so many others, all enjoying the thrill of their new beginnings. I step into the circle, and a rush of energy shoots me upward.

Finally, I can be with my parents again.

Printed in the United States
67602LVS00003B/1-69

9 781413 777376